WAITING TO RUN

OSWALD

An Ozzie Rabbit Mystery

W.H. Matlack

Cover Art:
Don Ramie

http://ramie.net/

Publisher's Note:

This is a work of fiction. All names, characters, places, and events are the work of the author's imagination.

Any resemblance to real persons, places, or events is coincidental.

Solstice Publishing - www.solsticepublishing.com

Waiting to Run

by

W.H. Matlack

Dedication

For my wife, Joan,

and of course Dorothy

NOVEMBER, 1965 – DOROTHY

Dorothy Kilgallen was sitting comfortably in her favorite lunchtime booth. Her fur collar kept her skinny shoulders protected from the chill emanating from P. J. Clarke's always-running air conditioning. Dorothy was always cold. Her Cobb salad was barely touched, but two empty vodka and tonic glasses cluttered her place at the table. Clarke's was filled with the sounds of glasses tinkling, low conversation, the clack of high heels on the polished floor, and waiters asking the usual questions waiters always ask patrons.

As she finished sipping her third vodka and tonic, she lit a cigarette, turned her head, and blew a lung-full of acrid smoke towards the wall where it bounced off and joined the hazy cloud built up from an entire evening of people doing the same. She then looked demurely over the rim of her glass at her agent, Don Krismont, and said. "In five more days I'm going to bust this case wide open." She put the glass down, and stirred it a bit with a well-manicured finger—a bad habit that made Don look away for a moment in embarrassment.

They had been talking about her investigative work on the JFK assassination, still very much on the public's mind even after two years. Don Krismont, her agent, had no doubt that this was not an idle statement. In fact, Don couldn't remember a time when Dorothy had ever mentioned an investigative report she was working on before it was in print. Her diminutive appearance was misleading. Dorothy was one of the sharpest and most tenacious investigative reporters Don had ever known. She had proved her mettle time and time again in her early years on the *New York Evening Journal* posting brilliant stories on organized crime and politics. Nonetheless, Don was skeptical. The JFK investigation kept spewing out an endless amount of conspiracy theories, not to mention it was totally rife with inept investigations. Don firmly believed it should be laid to rest just as JFK's bullet-riddled body had been two years before. He sighed, took another sip from his martini and reflected for a moment on Dorothy, his most famous—and most lucrative—client.

In 1938 after having established herself as a first-rate investigative reporter, Dorothy's career took a turn onto Fame Street when she began writing the *Voice of Broadway*, a column focused on show business news and gossip. Even as a gossip columnist, her facts were always right on the money and her clear, sharp prose won an almost fanatic readership.

She had even supercharged her fame and popularity by winning a seat as a panelist on the sophisticated and overly formal television program, *What's My Line?*. It was an amazingly popular show for reasons Don never really understood. It was slow moving and pompous with that idiot host, Daly, and if he wasn't enough, there was always that cardboard cutout, Bennet Cerf, the pompous publisher of Random House.

Both always dressed in formal tuxedos for God's sake, and the female panelists all wore expensive gowns. It was like a prom for aging has-beens. Not only was the show pompous, it was totally predictable. Don thought of it as the show where absolutely nothing ever happened. Whenever Don watched it, always from the front row in the audience section, he wanted to yell out, "He's a God dammed *plumber* for Christ sake." It was unbelievably tedious, but there you go. A big part of being an agent was pretending to like everything your client was involved in. Or as Daly would state it, "Everything *in which* your client is involved."

On that show, Dorothy easily out-performed her fellow panelists in questioning guests to determine their professions. Each question could only be answered by a "yes" or "no," and each "no" answer added five dollars to the contestant's winnings, with a fifty-dollar top prize if the profession wasn't guessed. A whole fifty bucks! Imagine that! The panelists could keep asking questions until a "no" answer was received and then questioning moved to the next panelist. Dorothy was sometimes criticized for asking questions that she knew would be answered with a "yes" to increase her on-camera time, and Daly, the program's host, was rumored to have once referred to her as "that chinless wonder." Great stuff, that. Too bad he couldn't spread *that* juicy gossip around.

However, she proved to have the best track record among all the panelists for guessing a contestant's profession. The show was extremely popular, and it made Dorothy a household name. Meanwhile, in New York she continued to be one of the best-read columnists.

After Dorothy's statement about blowing the lid off of the JFK investigation, she clammed up and wouldn't give Don any more insight, but Don was able to read a lot by her expression and overall bearing. She was excited and so full of adrenaline that she could barely sit still. On later reflection, Don thought that her downfall came because she was so full of herself that she thought nothing could happen to her. But investigating the JFK case was like running with the bulls at Pamplona.

NOVEMBER 7th and 8th, 1965 – DISCOVERY

Sunday, November 7th, 1965, Dorothy's last appearance on *What's My Line?* airs live. Was she slurring her words just a little? It was hard to tell. It certainly wasn't noticeable to the audience. They devotedly loved her ability to outshine the other panelists, which she did as usual that night by guessing three of the guests' professions. There were quite a few minor inconsistencies in her behavior that evening, but nothing that indicated she was depressed or even contemplating suicide.

After that show, Dorothy returned to her opulent Park Avenue condominium around 2:00 a.m. Monday morning, November 8th. At around 2:30 a.m. she called the manager of the Western Union office and asked him to send over a messenger to pick up her column and take it over to the *Journal-American*. She said it would be at the usual place "in the door" for pickup.

Dorothy had a busy morning planned for that Monday. First was a hair appointment at her townhouse, followed by a meeting at her son's school scheduled for 10:30 a.m.

Her hair stylist arrived at 8:45 a.m., used a key Dorothy had given him and went up to the third floor bedroom and into the small dressing room where Dorothy always had her hair done.

Dorothy wasn't in the dressing room and her hairdresser noticed that the air conditioner was on even though it was cold outside. He plugged in his curling irons and entered the bedroom to find Dorothy sitting up in bed.

"Dorothy," he said softly. "Are we ready?"

Dorothy didn't move. That was very unsettling. He moved closer thinking she might still be sleeping. She wasn't. She was dead.

There were several things that just didn't seem right to her hairdresser. First, Dorothy never used the third-floor bedroom, sleeping instead on the fifth floor. Her husband slept on the fourth. The third floor bedroom wasn't her room or her bed. It was where she got her hair and makeup done. It was her own styling station.

Second, instead of being dressed in old socks and pajamas as she usually was on Monday mornings, she was fully dressed as though she was planning to go out. Her wig was on, false eyelashes in place, full makeup. None of this was right for going to bed.

And then the air conditioner… it was on; yet it was cold outside, and Dorothy always complained of being cold. In fact, it was a cold enough night that the heat should have been on. The hairdresser rang for the butler and as he was waiting for him to arrive, he noticed a sheet of paper lying on the floor where it had been pushed under the door. He didn't get a chance to read what was on it.

When the hairdresser left Dorothy's townhouse later that morning, he noticed a police car with two officers in it. They ignored him, and he didn't approach them to discuss Dorothy's death. Police detectives only showed up later that day—after an announcement was made on CBS News.

Her autopsy showed death by a combination of alcohol and barbiturates under undetermined circumstances. The piece of paper was never found. As to Dorothy's comment that she would "blow open" the JFK case, her husband stated that piece of journalism would go with her to her grave.

MONDAY MORNING, NOVEMBER 8TH, 1965 - THE HOT POTATO

New York PD Detective Lieutenant Brad Small and his partner, Detective Rodney Goodwin, were ordered to investigate the suspected suicide at Kilgallen's Park Avenue condominium later the afternoon of her death.

Small thought it curious that they should be called in so late in the day, but the chief was certain that the case was a suicide and therefore not urgent—if you consider most of the mayhem that goes down in New York on a weekend—especially one so close to Thanksgiving. There was no mention of a connection to the JFK assassination, and besides, the Medical Examiner had finished his initial diagnosis of suicide due to the presence of alcohol and barbiturates. Small always held the conclusion that MEs were primarily concerned with the mechanical causes of death and had very little concern with the social causes. That was the detective's job.

A detective for ten years now, Small was a family man with three children at home, all teenagers—a boy and two girls. His oldest, Brad Junior, was seventeen and in the process of deciding to follow in his dad's footsteps and join the academy right after high school. Small felt that would make a very good career choice for the boy, but he would need to understand, as much as possible, what it was really like.

Small felt it was his responsibility to provide as much guidance as possible to the boy, and surprising for a teenager, Brad, Jr. agreed, and the two set up a standing appointment right after dinner to spend an hour or so, just the two of them, discussing the realities of what police work was like. As a result, Small would do just about anything to be able to get home for dinner on time and spend the precious hour with his son.

Not surprisingly, Goodwin asked if they could stop for a cup of coffee—in a to-go cup of course—before going to the scene. Goodwin often bragged that he could live on caffeine alone, and Small didn't doubt it one bit. The trouble was that the stop would be just one more delay in getting home on time.

The detectives reached the death scene around mid-afternoon. They were warned not to call it a crime scene because Miss Kilgallen's fame might cause a hysterical reaction in the press that would go far beyond a suicide story. In fact, celebrity suicides in New York were common enough that they usually only occupied a small section of the front page for a day or two. The first day generally carried the news itself—where she was found; how she did it; comments from friends, relatives, and agents—that kind of thing. If the person were important enough, the second day of editorial would consist of a look back at the person's career. Day three, the person would be totally forgotten as the spotlight turned to some other unfortunate individual.

A mysterious murder of a famous person, on the other hand, would be treated (in the New York papers at least) with all the drama of a Broadway play. Reporters would milk the story sometimes for years. And right in the middle of the whole mess would be the NYPD. So, they had been cautioned to be careful with their comments and to remember—it was *most likely* a suicide or accidental death, and not to read something into it that wasn't really there.

The vast majority of homicide calls took Detective Small and his partner into seamy walk-up flats in New York's poverty-stricken neighborhoods, but once in a while somebody rich and famous died under mysterious circumstances. Even though he hated admitting it, even to himself, he always got a bit of a thrill knowing he had full access to those previously forbidden quarters. But, examining how the other half lived was not his job. It was clearly examining how the other half died, and generally there was very little difference between a "better half death" and a "John Doe death." They were both ugly.

Dorothy's Park Avenue townhouse was a neat, five-story brick building with three windows looking out from each row. It was a classic New York townhouse—stylish without being imposing. It looked secure, too, with its substantial black metal door.

Curiously, there was no police guard at the front door. That in itself was a statement that inside was no crime scene beyond a simple suicide. Goodwin, still juggling his coffee, opened the door without knocking, and the two detectives entered the darkened hallway. Hearing the front door open, a face appeared at the top of the stairs. It was one of the crime-scene techs, a younger one. Only been working with the department for a few months. Small thought his name was Bruce or something like that.

"Come on up, guys," he said. "Looks like we got a suicide on the third floor."

Small wiped his shoes on the sisal mat and entered the foyer. As Goodwin dutifully wiped his own feet, Small paused for a moment inside to take in the atmosphere—kind of like a dog would do with its sensitive nose. The mechanics of the death would be analyzed and recorded by him and others, but not the overall atmosphere. That really wasn't a good name for it, but Small didn't have anything better in mind.

The atmosphere would help answer questions like: what kind of people lived here; what the surroundings said about them; what kind of choices they made in decorating, choosing paintings, and other art pieces; what would it be like to live here day after day. Small knew that home was a special place because it was the only space in a person's life where the surroundings were totally chosen by the people who lived there. Ultimately, answering these questions would help answer the big questions, why did someone die here? And how did it happen?

Moving through the tastefully decorated foyer, Small was once again taken with the contrast in people's lives. The house reminded him more of a small museum than a home. Or at least the kind of home he lived in. Contrasts between Small's life and Dorothy's were everywhere. The floors were some kind of a highly polished wood—very dark in color with a beautiful grain. Expensive-looking oriental rugs were tastefully scattered about. It made him wonder just how much Dorothy really had to do with all the decisions. He guessed she hired an expensive decorator, gave him or her some general instructions, and then turned her attention to her career.

In contrast, Small's working-man's brownstone across the river in Brooklyn featured practical linoleum—the best choice for a growing, energetic family like his. His three boys could pretty much spill anything they liked on the floor, and his wife, Sally, could mop it up in a jiffy with a damp paper towel, although he mopped up plenty of spills himself. He and Sally tried to share as much of the mundane housework as possible.

The linoleum pattern was carefully chosen by Sally with exhaustive approvals from Sally's female friends. That kind of involvement really made a family feel as though they had made a home rather than jobbing it out to a so-called professional. He wondered what it was like for Dorothy's three children growing up in such formal surroundings.

Another set of stairs and the two detectives reached the third floor where one of the building's three bedrooms was located. They approached the bed carefully. Dorothy was sitting up slightly propped against the pillows. She looked remarkably good for a corpse. Small noticed that all her makeup was in place. Even her false eyelashes were still on. The only thing really amiss was her wig that was slightly askew.

As Small approached the bed he began the little litany in his head that he always did: "Tell me. Tell me what happened to you."

The ME was standing by the bed. He'd been waiting for the detectives to arrive so he could go back to his office to begin the autopsy and then, maybe, get home at a decent hour today. He wasn't impressed with celebrities. It wasn't that they drew the press like flies to spilled milk. He always liked the glare of camera lights and the bulbs flashing. Each strobe just underscored his importance to the city. Even though the police always seemed to get more press attention than he did, he always felt that he was the true detective in every homicide case, because he was the one who determined the all-important cause of death. The police were there only to determine who or what created the cause of death. More of a quasi-scientific process, really, than his task. But the press only wanted to hear that cause of death from him, and then they moved on to the police investigation.

Of course a full autopsy would be required before he could push the victim back into the cold storage locker for the last time and move onto the next case. He always looked forward to the autopsy because it was pure science, and if performed correctly, unassailable in the courtroom— if a bit under appreciated by the press.

The ME greeted Small, "Good afternoon detective Small," and with a cursory glance at Goodwin, "Detective Goodwin."

"Hello, Doctor Massaro," Small returned the greeting. "What do you think?"

"About Miss Kilgallen here, or about the Yankees' failure to make the World Series?" Massaro said with a completely straight face.

"Let's start out by discussing Miss Kilgallen, and then, if we have time, we can dissect the Yankees' season," retorted Small with an equally straight face.

"Okey doke," said Massaro. "At face value, I'd say the young lady succumbed to a nasty little cocktail consisting of alcohol and prescription barbiturates, which, by the way, seems to be the preferred way to end one's life if one is wealthy enough to afford very expensive Scotch." With his rubber gloves still on his hands, Massaro picked up a bottle of Dalmore. "We're talking twenty or thirty thou a bottle here," he said as he held the half empty bottle up to the lamp. "Do you know how very tempting it is to have just a shot of this? I mean… there would be plenty left for…"

"Death by virtue of drugs and expensive liquor?" Small interrupted. For his part, Massaro shook his head, frowned and carefully placed the bottle back on the nightstand exactly where it was. Small figured there would be at least one shot missing by the end of the day.

"I don't think I can buy that from you just now, doctor. Aren't we getting just a little ahead of ourselves here? I mean suicide based on some casual evidence carefully laid out to support that conclusion? Doesn't just about every killer who dispatches someone with drugs and alcohol try to make it look like suicide?"

"Perhaps, detective, but she was in full makeup with her wig on and all," said the doctor. "Women are vain. They are certainly motivated to look their best. At all times, mind you, even the last time anyone will ever look at them. If it were a mistaken overdose, wouldn't she have prepared herself for bed? Wouldn't a woman like Dorothy here have taken time to scrub off her makeup so as not to soil her expensive sheets, removed her uncomfortable false eyelashes, taken off her wig, you know, the whole nine yards? And if she was somehow forced to consume it all, wouldn't there be some sign of a struggle?"

"OK, we'll use suicide as a working conclusion, but I'll need to speak to a few people before I sign off on it," Small said. "For starters, who discovered her?"

"It was her hairdresser, a Mr. Marc Sinclaire."

"How do you spell that, and where might I find Mr. Sinclaire now?"

"S-I-N-C-L-A-I-R-E. Evidently he waited around for a while to be interviewed, and then went home," said Massaro. "You guys did take your time getting here."

"Yes… well, I still need to speak to him," Small said. "Anyone bother taking down his address?"

"I'm sure you'll be able to find it in Ms. Kilgallen's address book there next to her phone," said Massaro.

Small gave Goodwin a glance and a nod of his head, and gestured toward the nightstand and the French-style phone that stood on it. It was white with gold trim. Goodwin took a final swig of his coffee and started to place the empty cup on the stand, but caught himself just in time. Small thought to himself, "What a freaking mess."

"Alright, Dr. Massaro," Small said. "Give me a tour of the body."

WHO, WHAT, WHERE AND WHY?

Now Small entered the mechanical part of the investigation. Any violent death promised to reveal a lot of clues, the more violent the death, the more clues. Small tried to open himself to both facts and impressions. He kept several questions in mind: Who was this person on the bed? What kind of life did she lead? What went wrong? Why would she kill herself, or why would another person take the risk to kill her? Was it someone she knew? Someone she trusted? How hard was it to get close to her to perform the act? Did it excite the killer? Did the killer show signs of being enraged, or was he or she just conducting business for someone?" Each question answered brought Small that much closer to the truth, and the truth always led directly to the killer.

They approached the body in silence. Small had seen photos of Dorothy, and being a fan of "What's My Line?" he had seen her many times on television. In fact, he had watched her last show just hours before she died. On the grainy black and white television in Small's home, she seemed very small in stature—almost unnoticeable among the other panelists. But as soon as she began questioning the guests, her skills in deductive reasoning came out. It was always more fun watching Dorothy than the other panelists who all seemed to just bumble through the questioning compared to Dorothy. Even with her blindfold on, Dorothy seemed to look right through it like a spotlight in a prison break.

There wasn't much at stake, of course. Just fifty bucks if you stumped all the panelists. Maybe that was part of the appeal of the show, but nonetheless some of the brighter contestants could be seen becoming a bit uncomfortable with Dorothy's honing in on the truth. In fact, during the last show, Dorothy was as much on her game, so-to-speak, as ever having nailed three contestants with a minimum of questions. She certainly didn't project any negative "vibes" during the show that would indicate a suicide planned for later that evening.

Small had investigated enough suicide cases to know they were usually planned many weeks in advance. The victim would go through endless dialogue with her or himself over his or her situation and how hopeless it was. After a lot of thought leading to the conclusion that he or she was better off dead, thoughts would turn to the logistics of how to perform the deed. This would require a lot of time weighing the pros and cons of each method within reach of the victim: a gun (where to obtain one in a city like New York, and then, of course, where to place the shot); throwing himself in front of a train (extraordinarily dramatic, but unacceptably painful, and it leaves a mutilated corpse not to mention how it inconveniences a lot of people); jumping off a bridge/drowning (not a lot of pain, and an acceptable corpse, but a hassle to get to the jumping off point—not to mention uncomfortable in the late fall or winter season).

That led to poison. Painful substances like rat poison would inflict too much punishment and probably leave an ugly, contorted expression (unacceptable for a beautiful lady). The only method acceptable to a lady like Dorothy was most likely either an overdose of sleeping pills or the civilized combination of liquor and barbiturates. You drift off into forever land and leave a beautiful corpse—all dressed up for viewing as was the case with lovely Dorothy here.

So that was all consistent with the lady lying on the bed here, but it wasn't consistent with Dorothy's behavior over the past few weeks. With all that going on in her mind, she would have seemed preoccupied, distracted, morose, depressed, and even temperamental. She wouldn't have been able to put those thoughts out of her mind, not completely anyway. Small felt that he would have seen just a trace of it during her last performance: A small hesitation before forming a question; a slightly pained expression when being introduced; just anything like that, but she was as smooth as silk—on the show anyway. Small made a note to interview the people she encountered after the show. Like most live television or stage performers, he knew that she would most likely have gone somewhere for a late dinner, or a drink. Or just to be seen one last time.

AS THOUGH SHE HAD PEACEFULLY FALLEN ASLEEP

With these thoughts completed, Small moved closer to the bed. Dorothy was lying on top of the covers wearing a blue matching peignoir and robe. It wasn't exactly a warm outfit, especially considering that the air conditioner was on. He turned to the ME. "Was that AC on when the body was discovered?"

"Nothing has been touched," Massaro replied.

"So then it was on?"

"Yes, yes, it was on," Massaro answered. He tried not to appear irritated with these detailed questions the police always asked. His only concern was how the person died. Not why.

"Doesn't that seem a little suspicious to you?" Small said. "I mean, she's hardly dressed, and it's cold outside." Smith glanced at Goodwin, who made a note in the little casebook he always carried with him.

Small thought about it for a minute, and turned to Goodwin. "Look, Rod, why don't you split your notebook into a suicide and murder section. We've got pretty strong elements of both going on here."

"OK," Goodman said. "Air conditioning in the murder column. Negligee in which column?"

"I'd say the suicide column," Small replied. "If she was worried about being cold during the night, she probably would have put on some warm pajamas. We'll need to talk to her husband about what she could be expected to wear on a night like this. We'll have to ask him about the AC, too. Do we know where he is right now?"

"Yes, he's upstairs in his bedroom waiting to be called."

"So, everyone's has their own bedroom?"

"Looks that way."

Small bent over Dorothy to get a closer look at her face and makeup. You really wouldn't call her a beautiful woman. More like pretty. Her makeup and wig were designed to make the most of her looks, and everything was age-appropriate. Her wig was slightly askew, which spoiled the overall look a bit, but the rest of her makeup looked like it could have been applied by Dorothy.

"What's going on, Dorothy?" Small said to himself. "What are you trying to tell us?" She smelled slightly of a powder of some sort. Rose came to Small's mind for no good reason. There was no unpleasant death smell as yet. He bent closer to her lips. The smell of Scotch was strong.

There was a book on the bed just out of her reach. It was turned upside down, which wouldn't have been the case if she had been reading it while waiting for death to come. Of course, she might have been reading it, and then put it down as she began feeling the effects coming on...

No reading glasses were anywhere in sight, either. Small stifled a chuckle at that phrase. Then he noticed the book's title, *Murder One* by Dorothy Kilgallen. It seemed to be too obvious to be a last minute warning. There were no other books in this room, which indicated that she would have had to bring it upstairs with her or have gone to another room to retrieve it. Probably down to the first floor where Small had noticed some expensive-looking, leather-bound volumes in a bookcase. *Murder One* was bound with standard cotton wrapped in a paper dust jacket, but it was *her* book. Small wasn't sure what it meant. It was like the wig...just out of place enough to be a clue, but a clue to what?

If she could have moved around that much, didn't it stand to reason that she could have evaded a killer? Or at least put up signs of a struggle.

The presence of the book didn't make any sense at all to Small. Who takes a lethal dose of barbs and drinks half a bottle of outrageously expensive Scotch, and then tries to read a book, especially your own book? Maybe Dorothy was taking stock of her past accomplishments. A last look back at life and at something she was proud of. He didn't think she had written another book. He'd have to check on that. Anyway, the book was evidence—of what he wasn't completely sure. Fingerprints wouldn't yield any real evidence. Many people could have handled that book.

No, he didn't think a victim would try to concentrate on reading a book before death took over. You would probably just lie back and wait for bliss. And pray that you weren't making a mistake. Wasn't Dorothy Catholic?

"Goodwin," Small said without looking up. "Upside down book in murder column. No reading glasses in the same column. Double check to see if she needed them. Also put religion in that category and make a note to find out what religion she was if any."

Small stood up and did a slow turn around the room. Nothing out of place. No sign of a struggle. No sign of a note, either. He'd have to check the rest of the house for one. It could be anywhere, but again, if one existed, it could be forged to be intentionally misleading, or it could be the definitive clue of suicide.

"Goodwin, we'll need to interview the hairdresser and the husband. Meanwhile, put down 'a lack of preoccupation' in the murder column. In the suicide column add, 'no sign of struggle.' No, make that 'no apparent sign of struggle.' Also, put 'no note' down in a new category marked "uncertain."

Once again Small took in the room as a whole, only this time he walked around the perimeter very slowly. Occasionally he would issue a statement to Goodwin, like: "I want that AC dusted—especially the on/off switch. Mark the temp it's set at, too. First thing in the morning call the power company and see if they can tell from a spike in electricity usage when it might have been turned on. Oh, and by the way, I've changed my mind on how to list the AC. I think it should go in the suicide column, don't you? I mean if she was so vain as to check out in full makeup, wouldn't she want the room as cold as possible to slow up the decay factor?"

"That's a good thought, detective," said Goodwin. "Into the suicide column it goes."

"Is her husband still in the house?" asked Small. "If so, let's get him down to the first floor and have a friendly little chat with him."

A LITTLE CHAT WITH THE HUS

Richard Kollmar, Dorothy's husband, was a former radio actor who, back in the thirties, had played the popular Boston Blackie on the radio program of the same name. By all accounts his union with Dorothy was a happy one. Back in 1945 they even hosted a live radio program together called *Breakfast with Dorothy and Dick*. Yes, Dorothy got top billing, but that was fine with Dick. He could see that her sharp intelligence and writing ability would take her far beyond where his stiff acting talents would.

Dorothy's wide range of talents did kick in, and by the beginning of the 1950's her column was running in nearly two hundred newspapers across the country. Dick had happily taken a supporting role in their partnership. He mostly stayed out of the way when he wasn't needed and reliably showed up when he was.

Small told the ME to wrap Dorothy up and process her, and, relieved, the ME and his assistants began the "bagging and tagging" process. Small didn't need to participate in that, so he and Goodwin went down to the first floor. They arranged three stuffed chairs in a small circle next to the highly polished piano and waited for "Dick" to join them. One of the uniformed cops went upstairs to summon him.

"He really likes being called Dick?" asked Goodwin.

Small just looked up at him from his notes.

Changing the subject, Goodwin ran his hand over the top of the piano. "Look. Not a speck of dust," he said. "Do you suppose anyone even plays it? It's a Steinway, too."

"There are probably hundreds of objects in this house that no one touches. They're all there to give a distinct impression of success and wealth," Small said. "No one really cares about any of them. It's the definition of the word, "possession." When you are rich and famous, you possess something like that just because you can and because it's expected of you. It's the things a person really loves that tell us the most about him… or her."

"Yeah. Like that movie, *The Cain Mutiny,* with that sled. What was it called? Snowflake or something like that."

"Okay. You're thinking about the movie, *Citizen Kane*, and the sled was called *Rosebud*," said Small.

"Yeah. That's it. Rosebud. Haw! What a laugh. All that stuff, and the guy just mooned over a sled."

After that exchange, things got a little boring for Goodwin at least. Small's mind was busy trying to sort out how someone would have been able to get into the house and up to the third floor to dose Dorothy all the while with Dick asleep on the fifth floor.

Goodwin wandered around the formal room gawking at fine porcelain figures and formal photos of Dorothy and the many famous people she knew. There were just two photos of her and Dick. One taken as they broadcast one of their breakfast shows years ago, and a formal photo of the two of them taken recently.

About fifteen minutes went by before they heard Dick descending the stairs. As he appeared, he looked properly distraught. His eyes were red and puffy. He had on a silk robe that looked carefully wrinkled, and he was unshaven.

As he reached the landing, Small said, "Mr. Kollmar, we're very sorry for your loss, but we need to ask you a few questions before we go. Would that be alright with you?"

"Yes, of course," Dick replied. "I'm happy to cooperate in any way I can."

"Good," said Small. "Please have a seat here by the piano." Everyone took a seat. The two detectives were directly across from Dick and separated by about four feet, so that he would have to turn his head to answer questions from each one. That way, if he were talking to Small, Goodwin could observe his body language and vice versa. It wasn't as good as a one-way mirror, but it was effective.

"Mr. Kollmar, could you please tell me what you were doing last night?" Small started the process.

"Well, certainly," said Kollmar. "Dorothy had a show in the evening as she does every Sunday night. She always gets a little nervous about the show, so… uh, typically I stay out of her way."

"Out of her way?" said Goodwin. Much of Goodwin's role in the interview was to simply repeat a witness's statements. That always had the effect of causing them to provide more information relative to the statement. It was a standard technique. It also forced the witness to turn and look at Goodwin.

"That's right," said Kollmar. "She needs to be able to clear her mind while making numerous decisions before the show."

"Decisions?" asked Small. Dick's head swiveled back again to Small. Goodwin had a bit of difficulty stifling a chuckle as he thought of Dick's head turning. He kept thinking of the word "Dickhead."

"Yes decisions," said Dick.

"What kind of decisions?" said Goodwin. Back swiveled the head.

"Well, first of all, it's a very formal show, so she needs to pick out a formal gown. And it can't be one that she has recently worn. So, she has to keep track of that. And then there's the wig… er, hairstyle. She has to discuss that with her hairdresser."

"Who is her hairdresser?" said Small. The head again.

"Her hairdresser? You don't know him? He found her. He was the one who…" Tears welled up in Dick's eyes. He couldn't go on.

"It's OK," Goodwin said. He looked down at his notes and turned a page pretending that he wasn't sure of the answer. "Is it Mr. Marc Sinclaire? Was he her hairdresser?"

"Yea… yes," Dick managed to choke out. He pulled a monogrammed handkerchief out of his pocket, and used it to daub at his eyes.

"So what was Mr. Sinclaire's relationsh… I mean role with Dorothy?" asked Small. The head kept looking down. The hands fiddled with the robe's silken tie.

"Of course he took care of her wigs and also did her hair when she chose not to wear one," said Dick.

"Were they close, Mr. Kollmar?" said Goodwin. The head moved up and swiveled to Goodwin.

"Close? What do you mean close? I don't understand that question," said Dick. The hands tightened around the tie, and Dick's body went tense for an instant. Goodwin noticed a touch of anger in his eyes.

"Well, really, most women seem to develop close relationships with their hairdressers. They can be almost like therapists. There's nothing for a woman to do but relax and talk during the process, and the stylist usually listens to everything. I know my wife chats away with her hairdresser for the entire time. She comes back full of gossip that she is just dying to tell me…" Goodwin caught a glance from Small and stopped talking.

Dick looked at Goodwin for a moment. It looked like he was trying to tell if there was a nasty insinuation to the question. "Yes. I guess you could call them close friends. They talked mostly about the entertainment world. Sometimes Dorothy would pick up a lead from Sinclaire that she could follow up on and work into her column. He was well connected."

"Let's talk a bit more about last night," said Small. "Was there anything out of the usual that you noticed?"

"Well, accounting for my evening… I guess that's what you really want to know about, right?"

"That'll be an excellent start," said Small.

"OK. Dorothy had a show last night as she did every Sunday. As I already mentioned she was kept pretty busy in the late afternoon selecting gowns, etcetera. I already went over that. I would stay out of the way by going up to my bedroom…"

"Your bedroom?" asked Small. "Which room was your bedroom?"

"My bedroom is on the fourth floor."

"Did Dorothy usually sleep on the third floor – where she was found this morning?"

Dick fixed his gaze on the floor. "No… she usually slept on the fifth floor bedroom."

"You didn't sleep together…"

"No, detective, we only slept together when we… she was a light sleeper, and I tend to snore—or so I've been told."

"So she was usually sleeping on the fifth, and you were usually one floor below her. So your snoring wouldn't disturb her. Is that right, Mr. Kollmar?"

"Yes, that's usually the case, detective." Dick stood up and walked over to a small bar behind the piano. "Would either of you care for something to drink?" he said as he poured a scotch and tinkled two ice cubes into the glass. Small noticed it was the same brand as the bottle next to Dorothy.

Small caught Goodwin's eye. The irony wasn't lost between either of them. "No, sir," Goodwin said. "We're on du…"

"Yes, yes. Of course," Dick said. "You're on duty. No drinking when you're on duty. I understand." He sauntered back to his chair, stood behind it placing his left hand on the back of it, and took a healthy, almost loving swig of the scotch, and then held it up to the light. "You

28

know what I appreciate most about a good scotch?" he asked. "It's the color, the beautiful amber color. Nothing quite compares with it."

"Please take your seat again, Mr. Kollmar. We've only a few more questions for you. I know it's been a very stressful morning for you," said Small. Dick sat, took another swig and placed the half-empty glass on top of the piano. No coaster. This disregard for a fine piece of furniture—which is all the piano really was to these people—made Small squirm.

"Where were we?" Dick asked. "Oh, yes. What was *I* doing all evening? Well, *I* took a nap upstairs, watched the news and then got dressed to attend Dorothy's show. I then dutifully sat in the front row right next to that asshole agent of hers and suffered through another half hour of formal bullshit with the rest of America. I then came home by myself, got plastered, and went to bed."

"Did you remember hearing anything out of the ordinary?" asked Small.

"No. Nothing. Evidently my snoring covers most sounds."

"Did you hear Dorothy come home?"

"Yes, I think so. About 11:30."

"Did she greet you or say anything to you?"

"No, she always comes in and then goes off to write her column. That's the most important thing. It has to be shipped to the paper before four, or at some ungodly hour. I'm not really sure which."

"Are you sure of the time?"

"The time? After a few of these—he grabbed the scotch from the piano and held it up—I'm not sure of anything. That's why I like them. It's very rare stuff, by the way. You wouldn't believe how much a single bottle costs. But once you get used to the finer stuff—there's no going back. No. No going back." Dick took a healthy swig and placed the glass back on the wet ring on the piano.

"When did you become aware of your wife's demise?" Small asked.

"When Marc came upstairs and shook me awake," Dick answered.

"That's Mr. Sinclaire?" asked Small.

"Yes, yes. Of course, Mr. Sinclaire. Mr. Marc Sinclaire. Dorothy's hairdresser." The scotch seemed to be bringing on a disagreeable mood. "Well," Small thought, "It can't be much fun being questioned like this just after your wife has died."

"After Mr. Sinclaire woke you up, did you go downstairs to see Dorothy?"|

"Good God, no! Why would I want to do that? It was upsetting enough when Mar… er, Mr Sinclaire told me she was dead. I didn't doubt him about that. I certainly didn't want to see her."

"What did you do upon hearing the news, then?"

"Ha! Well, I poured myself a stiff one and just waited."

"Waited?"

"Yes, waited."

"For what exactly, Mr. Kollmar?"

"For you, I guess, and all these questions. I needed to keep my head straight, and I knew I couldn't do that after seeing her… like that."

"So… you had more scotch?"

"Yes, I had more scotch. It clears my head."

"OK, Mr. Kollmar, I have just one more question for you," said Small. "Do you know of anyone who might have wanted your wife dead? For any reason no matter how crazy it sounds?"

"There was just one thing. I didn't think too much about it at the time, but there was that JFK assassination thing."

"Assassination thing?"

"Yes." Dick looked up and fixed his gaze on Small. "She said she was working on blowing the case wide open. Wide open is what she said."

"The JFK assassination case."

"Yes. She was working on a book or an article— something. I'm never really sure what she works on. She has a strict policy of never showing anything in progress to anyone. Certainly not to me."

"So, why would that pose a danger to her? Working on that case, I mean. Wasn't the Warren Commission report the final word on it? That came out, when, about a year ago didn't it?"

"I'm sorry. I don't know any more about it. There have been a lot of theories; government involvement, that sort of thing. I really can't..." Dick swallowed the rest of his drink and began staring at the floor.

"OK, Mr. Kollmar," said Small. "I want to thank you for your cooperation. If you don't mind, we may have some follow-up questions for you over the next day or two."

Dick just shifted his gaze to one of the windows that looked out on Park Avenue. "I know nothing about all that JFK stuff. You hear me? Nothing!"

NOVEMBER 9th, 1965 - DOROTHY'S BFF

Small decided he and Goodwin had had enough for the day. "Goodwin, let's knock off for today, but before you go, I'd like you to recover Dorothy's address book up on the third floor. Then call Mr. Marc Sinclaire and try to arrange an interview time with him tomorrow down at headquarters."

They were both distracted for a moment by the ME's assistants carrying Dorothy's body down the stairs. They kept bumping the stainless steel gurney frame against the highly polished railing. Finally they made it all the way down the stairs and were able to extend the wheels. As the gurney was rolled across the floor, one of the wheels wobbled like a bad grocery cart. Both detectives watched the gurney until it was once again picked up by the assistants and carried down the steps and through the front door where it disappeared from view into the evening light.

Goodwin had set up an interview time with Sinclaire for 10 a.m. the next day, Tuesday, November 9th. Sinclaire arrived half an hour before the scheduled interview time. He was fashionably dressed in a gray, linen suit with a dark blue shirt and meticulously folded handkerchief in his coat pocket that matched his light blue tie. His thick, grey hair was carefully cut to be fashionably just a bit too long. Most women who saw him for the first time thought, "handsome," and then immediately wondered, "gay?"

Goodwin met Sinclaire in the waiting room. After shaking hands, Sinclaire said, "Thanks for asking me down here. I was beginning to wonder if anyone but me even cared at all about poor Dorothy."

"It's our job to care, Mr. Sinclaire," Goodwin said. "And we do care, believe me. In fact more than just care about what happened to Dorothy, it's our job and sworn duty to find out what happened to her. And we will, with your help."

As they entered one of the interview rooms, Goodwin asked Sinclaire if he would like something to drink. Sinclaire politely declined, and with those formalities over Goodwin began the interview by recording Sinclaire's personal information: age, residence, business, etcetera. Then they got down to business.

"Please describe what you found on the morning of November 8th, 1965," said Goodwin.

"Well, I came to Dorothy's townhouse to do her hair as I did every morning."

"What time was that?" asked Goodwin.

"I got there a little after noon, maybe around 12:15, or so."

"How did you gain access to the townhouse?"

"I've always been entrusted with a front door key."

"What happened after you entered the house?"

"I went directly up to the third floor, which is where I would do her hair. There's a little alcove up there, but she wasn't there as she usually was."

"Did you find this to be unusual?"

"Well, it had never happened before, but I didn't think much of it at first. I just plugged in the curlers and went to look for her."

"And where did you find her?"

"She was lying on the bed on that floor."

"The third floor?"

"Yes." Sinclaire removed the handkerchief from his pocket and wiped his eyes.

"Are you OK, Mr. Sinclaire?"

"Yes. I'm OK," The handkerchief was re-folded but remained in his hand.

"Can you continue?"

"Yes. I… I saw her on the bed, and I knew something was just wrong with her head."

"Wrong? How was her head wrong?"

"Well, you saw her yourself. It was at a weird angle, and she had her wig on. It was—I don't know—askew I guess is the best word. Askew. And she had all her makeup on—even her false eyelashes. She would never have gone to sleep with those on. Never!" Tears began running down his cheek. The handkerchief wiped again. "Unless she wanted to look her best for…" He began sobbing.

Small was uncomfortable with the sobbing. He understood masculine crying. It was always manifest as a kind of an inability to continue talking. The person would say he was sorry and then turn away. There was always a bit of choking, and then things would either resume, or the person would break off the conversation for a few minutes. But he had never seen a man sob.

And this was actual sobbing like a woman would do, totally distraught. "I'll get you some water," Small said, just to get out of the room. Goodwin looked up at him and made the "What? You're leaving me here?" gesture.

By the time Small got back with the water, the sobbing had mercifully ceased even though the handkerchief was in hand and ready just in case. Sinclaire took a grateful sip and thanked Small for the water.

"Outside of the makeup, did you notice anything else that wasn't right?" asked Small.

"Oh, you mean outside of her being dead and wearing makeup did I notice anything else?" Sinclaire said with just a hint of cynicism.

Small just stared at him without saying anything.

"Well, of course I'm not *trained* in this kind of thing, but it seemed odd that she was in the third floor bedroom. She never slept there that I know of," said Sinclaire.

"And you would know because…" Small led on.

"I would *know* because I did her hair nearly every day," said Sinclaire. "She always met me in the alcove, and she never slept in *that* bed. And I *don't* believe she killed herself. She was *not* depressed. In fact she was at the top of her game. Everyone was constantly asking her what she was planning to do next. She was always looking ahead, and people who are contemplating suicide do not look ahead."

"And you know all that because...." said Small.

"I know all that *because* I saw a cop being interviewed on TV. His job was to talk down jumpers—you know—off the bridge jumpers. He would always ask them what they had planned for tomorrow. Determined jumpers had no plans for the future, but those whom he had a chance of talking down could still look ahead."

"Anything else?" Small asked. He was beginning to slightly dislike Sinclaire's know-it-all attitude, but he conceded that he just might have a point.

"Look, Officer," said Sinclaire. "I don't mean to get pissy with you, but Dorothy was my best friend. I've known her for many years. We were closer than with any other people in our lives. And I'm getting the strong feeling that no one cares a hoot about what really happened to her. I mean I had left the townhouse long before you guys even showed up to investigate. What was with that?"

"Priorities, Mr. Sinclaire," said Small. "I don't need to tell you that it's a big city with a large number of awful things happening during the nights, especially weekend nights. We're short staffed in the homicide detective department, and this case was initially opened as a suspected suicide. I'm not saying that it is suicide, and that's why I'm talking to you. To help us all, and Dorothy in particular, find out what really happened here Sunday night. OK? So let's concentrate on Dorothy now."

"All right, detective," Sinclaire said. "The only other thing was that on my way out I saw a piece of paper on the floor just outside of the third floor bedroom. It was just a single sheet of standard-sized paper. Nothing was written on the side that I could see. I just left it because I didn't want to explain why I was messing with evidence. I don't know if it was important or not. Did your guys find it?"

Small glanced at Goodwin. Goodwin shook his head. "I'm not aware of anything like that being found. I'll look for it when I review the evidence back at the station," Small said. "So you knew her pretty well, then."

"Yes. I knew her *very* well," said Sinclaire. He looked Small right in the eye as he answered each question. Goodwin, whose job it was to read Sinclaire's body language during the interview, had the strong impression that he was hiding nothing and that he really did care for Dorothy as a friend would. How good a friend was hard to say at this point.

"How would you characterize your relationship?" asked Small.

"It was a professional relationship, but with a strong undercurrent of friendship. And, in case you are wondering, we were *just* friends. Very good friends, but nothing more," said Sinclaire.

"In your opinion did Dorothy use drugs?"

"Perhaps a few prescription drugs, maybe something to help her sleep, but nothing recreational or anything. To do what she did, she had to be as sharp as possible all the time."

"What about alcohol?" Sinclaire looked down at his hands for a moment.

"She liked going to clubs in the evenings or for lunch, but especially after her show. She would have a few drinks then, but I never saw her—what you would call drunk. She was always sober. Never slurred her words or bumped into anything."

"What about death threats? Did she ever receive any? Do you know of anyone who might want her dead? Or someone who would benefit in some way from her death?"

"Well, she did receive death threats over the years. She never took any of them seriously, although she always reported them to the police—more to establish a record of them than for the police to take them seriously and investigate. You could probably look into some of those.

"There was only one troublesome threat that I can remember," Sinclaire continued, "She was working on the JFK assassination case. She had been able to interview Jack Ruby—the only private interview Jack ever allowed. After that, she would talk about a book she was going to write. She said it would blow the lid right off the case. I think that might have made some people nervous, but no one took it seriously after the Warren Commission Report came out. You know. Lone gunmen. No conspiracy. All the real questions had been answered. As far as I know, she hadn't even started working on the book. After a while she stopped talking about it. Frankly, I can't believe people are still talking about conspiracies. You want to know what I think about the whole JFK conspiracy thing? " Sinclaire looked Small right in the eye again.

"That's what we're here to do. Find out what you think."

"Well, I think that the Federal Government is far too stupid to hide any conspiracy for more than five minutes. Look at what's already been leaked about Kennedy's involvement in Cuba—and with the Mafia. This whole thing was just two idiots acting alone. Two totally screwed up idiots who knew little more about life and politics than pulling a trigger. Were any of them involved in Dorothy's death? I just can't believe they were."

Sinclaire took a swig of water, then carefully put the mug down on the table—exactly (Goodwin noted) in the middle of the table. "Look," he continued, "What if there was some sort of government conspiracy involving Ruby? And what if Ruby confessed it to Dorothy? That he actually came out and said he was working for the CIA, or for the Russians, or for the Cubans, or for all of them… what if he confessed that to Dorothy? What if he said that he was under orders to make sure Oswald never talked? What's the worst that could happen? It couldn't be considered evidence. Ruby wasn't under oath during his little chat with Dorothy. There weren't any witnesses to it. And remember, Ruby has consistently denied that he was working for someone. As close as we were to each other, Dorothy never even told me what Ruby said to her during that interview. She would have said something to me. I'm just sure of it."

"So you think she was murdered, but not by the government or by foreign agents?" said Small.

"Sadly, I don't have any idea who killed her, or who even would benefit from her death. It's just a total, horrible mystery, and I wish you guys all the luck in the world solving it." Tears were beginning to well up in Sinclaire's blue eyes, but it didn't seem like another sobbing attack would follow. Sinclaire fixed his gaze on the mug for a moment, and then dragged it to the edge of the table where he gripped it with both hands so tightly that his fingers began turning white. Small knew he had given all the information he could at this time.

"Mr. Sinclaire, before you leave, I'd like you to sit down with detective Goodwin and give him a statement under oath about your whereabouts the morning of the eighth. We want to completely clear you as a suspect."

"I appreciate that," said Sinclaire. "I'll be happy to cooperate with detective Goodwin."

"Anything else you can think of to tell us?"

"No, but I do have a question for you. Dorothy asked me to deliver to her attorney a box of papers she kept in her office. When might I be allowed back in the house to do that?"

"Check with her husband tomorrow. I expect we'll clear the scene tonight."

"Tonight, huh?" said Sinclaire still staring at the empty mug. "You'll *clear* the scene tonight? Does that mean no more investigation? That you're done now?"

"Probably, but I can't say for sure at this moment," said Small. "The way it works is we'll present all the evidence to our chief, and he'll decide the case status. If I had to say at this point, I'd guess that the case would be determined a probable suicide under suspicious circumstances. It may remain an open case, or it may be closed. With no witnesses to the crime, and yes, suicide is a crime, no probable perpetrators, and most of the evidence supporting suicide, the chief will most likely be inclined to pull assets off the case."

"*Assets*," said Sinclaire. "Meaning you two."

"Yes."

After Sinclaire had gone, Small remained in the interview room with Goodwin to draft an alibi. He took out the notepaper he'd had Goodwin fill out at the crime scene. It read:

Murder
    Book (upside down – Dorothy's own book, *Murder One*)
      No reading glasses
      Religion (Catholic?)
      a lack of preoccupation
Suicide
      Make up/wig
      no *apparent* sign of struggle
Air conditioning (on)
Uncertain
No S note

He added, "No sign of depression" and "Future plans" to the murder list. It was inconclusive, but there were no leads in the murder section. No sign of break-ins or of intruders of any kind. She hadn't even ordered in a pizza. With absolutely no sign that anyone other than her husband had physical access to her, they would have to mark the file suicide under suspicious circumstances.

There was the husband, but there was no motive for him. As near as anyone could tell, he was allowed to spend as much money as he liked, so he wouldn't gain any greater access to her bank account if she were dead. In fact it was a joint account that had been checked out earlier that morning by the PD.

It seemed there was nothing left to do on this case except to bury poor Dorothy and allow the world to move on without her.

NOVEMBER 10th, 1965 - HUS AND BFF CLEAN UP

Early on the morning of the tenth, Marc Sinclaire rang the bell at the front door of Dorothy's townhouse. After years of using his key and walking right in, it seemed awkward to stand there waiting for a response from inside the house. For a brief moment he wondered what he would do if the bell wasn't answered. Would he use his key then? Given what he'd found the last time he used that key, he shuddered at the thought. That would be the most awkward situation of all, but he had made arrangements with Dorothy's husband to come over today and ferret out any personal papers or anything that might be embarrassing, so he fully expected the bell to be answered.

He still felt a kind of stiffness from Dorothy's death. That was the only word that seemed to define his emotions. He knew he was very much in mourning over Dorothy's death, and he felt a twinge of anger and frustration over how quickly the cops dismissed her case. He just knew deep inside that she had been murdered, but like the police, he couldn't fathom who would have done it… or how.

After a bit of brooding over that, he finally heard faint footsteps coming down the stairs. The noise stopped at the door, and Sinclaire knew he was being scrutinized via the little peephole screwed into the door. Finally came the metallic sounds of latches and chains being removed, and the door opened to reveal Richard "Dick" Kollmar, Dorothy's bumbling husband. Eight o'clock in the morning and Dick was already *sloshed*. He managed to slur out a "Good Morrow, Marc," before backing away from the entrance so Sinclaire could enter.

"Good God, Dick," Sinclaire said as he entered the darkened reception area. "Already?"

"Already wha?" Dick slurred back, the booze smell much stronger today than the furniture polish. Dick teetered a little bit holding on to the door for support. "Wha timeisit?"

"It's eight am, Dick, and we've got a lot of work to do. I'm going to need you to be able to open Dorothy's safe. Will you be able to do that, Dick?"

"For an ole pal like you?" Dick was really out of it. "I'll do anything fer you. An I thing you know that, too. Ole pal. Aneething. Ole pal."

Sinclaire had hoped Dick would be of some help since there was a mountain of papers to sort through. He had gotten glimpses of Dorothy's files and safe contents over the years, and she seemed to be the type who just kept everything under the guidelines of it being easier to save than to sort.

Somehow, the two of them made it up to Dorothy's office on the second floor. "Dick, just open the safe, please, and then you can lie down and take a nap, or something."

"No nap. Room spinning too much."

"Well then just write down the combination, and I'll open it."

"OK, pal. Anyting you say." Dick scribbled some numbers on a notepad on Dorothy's desk. He forgot to indicate right or left turns, but Sinclaire figured the sequence started with a right turn. Surprising to him, the combination worked the first time and the ancient safe opened with a protesting squeak. The safe was full nearly to the top with files, papers and small audiotape reels.

Dick sat down in Dorothy's chair and put his head down on her desk. A couple of minutes later, he was snoring and drooling. "Fucking pathetic," Sinclaire thought. Then he concentrated on his task.

The primary thing he was looking for were Dorothy's wills. He knew that her lawyer, Jon Smith possibly had current copies, but he wanted to make sure nothing important was left in the townhouse. Soon the relatives would descend and clean out the place. He began making piles of paper. First were contracts and other legal documents including what looked like her last will and testament. Assets were mostly given to Dick with generous gifts to her three children. Furniture and artwork were to be allocated to her children with Dick named to allocate them as he saw fit.

Contracts went in the legal pile, non-legal correspondence into the next pile. The biggest pile turned out to be notes and transcripts of interviews she had conducted. There were also about fifty, small audiotape reels.

It was noon before Sinclaire had sorted everything out and packed it all into a large box he'd brought with him. He labeled and marked it with Jon Smyth's name and address. According to Dorothy's instructions the lawyer was to keep all her notes and records for a period of fifty years, after which they could either be made public or destroyed—at her lawyer's discretion or whoever inherited his business.

Finished, he called a small messenger company to come pick up the boxes and walked over to where Dick was sleeping. Sinclaire gently woke him up. "Come on, Dick. Let's get you into the shower."

The box was picked up within an hour and delivered downtown to the law offices of Jon Smyth where it sat unopened for nearly fifty years.

PRESENT DAY - OLD CRAP

Richard Goldstein had a mistress. It wasn't a secret. There were no clandestine meetings after hours in discrete Manhattan hotels. His wife and daughter knew all about it. Also, there was no shame. But it was time to end it. It was time to finally close the law offices of Smyth and Goldstein and leave his mistress, the law, behind. Goldstein was done practicing law.

His wonderful, patient wife had plans for his retirement. A lot of plans, and none of them included practicing law. As she said to him, "Richard, you've been practicing law long enough that if you haven't figured out how to do it by now, you never will. It's time to quit."

Her comment actually wasn't all that funny. The law was like an ever-changing monster, and even the best lawyer could only master a small corner of it. For Smyth and Goldstein that meant managing the legal affairs of successful New York actors, authors, and other members of New York's illuminati. Richard had been privileged to meet and get to personally know a wide range of famous people over the years.

For the last time, Goldstein walked through the reception area and into his old office—the one he had shared with his senior partner, Jon Smyth, for over fifty years. Goldstein was young when Smyth hired him as an associate way back when. Young! That hardly expressed what he was. More like totally naive and knowing so little of how the law actually worked in the real world, the real world that Harvard Law School was definitely not.

It was through working for an actual firm that a young lion like Goldstein learned how to manipulate people and their agreements with others. Contracts were the heart and soul of what he did, and he knew how to break them when necessary and how to enforce them as well. He was very good at what he did, and that's why his name was on the door. Well, it wasn't actually on the door any longer, but if you looked closely at the frosted glass you could just barely make it out… like the ghost of Christmas past.

The firm was busy today, busy collapsing upon itself. Boxes were everywhere, and a constant stream of movers were coming in, excusing themselves as they brushed against the aging lawyer and expertly loading piles of boxes onto dollies and wheeling them out the door. The firm had been bought out by a rival firm engaged in the same area of the law, an uptown firm with an even more impressive list of clients than Smyth and Goldstein. But they were happy to add Smyth and Goldstein's modest list of loyal clients, and for a very fair price, too.

So, most of the boxes had that address on it, but occasionally, a workman would ask Goldstein where something or other should end up. Most of these boxes came from a small, private storage area just off the library. It was a place where the most sensitive case files were stored. They were mostly sensitive because they would reveal embarrassing secrets that his clients didn't want the world to know about—even clients who had died long ago. The files resulting from personal legal proceedings— paternity suits, embarrassing arrests, that sort of thing.

Just as he was about to leave, one of the workers wheeled out a very old-looking and musty box from the very depths of the storage area. "Sir, this is the last of the cold storage files. Where do you want it sent?"

The box was so covered with dust that Goldstein couldn't read the label. "Man, that is an oldie," he thought to himself. He took out a handkerchief and rubbed most of the dust off the label. It had faded so much that it was almost impossible to read. "Why weren't these labels placed on the front of these boxes instead so they wouldn't get totally buried in this awful dust?" Before replacing the kerchief, he folded it over and blew his nose into it. "Let's see what we have here," he said.

He took off his glasses and put his face so close to the label that he was immediately seized with a sneezing attack, and no clean handkerchief at hand. His wife came into the room and saved his dignity by digging out a tissue from her ubiquitous handbag. "Robert! What are you doing back here? Please let the workmen cart all this garbage out of here. Are you *trying* for an asthma attack?"

"No, I'm not. I just need to see what's written here. This looks like the oldest box…"

"Oldest and mustiest. Why would you even keep anything this long? Didn't it ever occur to you to weed out some of this junk once in a while?"

"No, dear. There was always too much current activity to bother…" His voice trailed off as he bent down for another close look at the curling label. "Hey, look," he said. "It says Dorothy Kilgallen. There could be anything in here. We need to take a close look…"

"*You* are not taking a close look at *anything* in here. Did it slip your mind that we are scheduled for a cruise in two days? You've got to pack and I need to do some more shopping, and yes, you're going to accompany me. I've lost you too many times to so-called *important* files."

"Well, dear, someone is going to have to go through the contents of this box. Dorothy was a very famous columnist, and there could be a lot of…"

"What's going on in here?" said Mary Goldburg, as she walked into the room. Mary was the Goldstein's only child. A homemaker from New Rochelle married to a stockbroker; she had zero interest in legal affairs, and was as anxious as her mother to extract her dad from the morass that she perceived the firm had become.

"Dad's getting hung up on an old box from the storage area," said Mrs. Goldstein.

"Good God. There was a storage area, too?" said Mary.

"Yes, and this musty old box was the oldest thing in it. Your dad wants to sift through the contents because some of them might be *valuable*."

"It has to be done," Goldstein said. "Someone's got to do it. We can't just toss it out."

"OK, here's what we can do," said Mary. "We'll ship it to San Francisco and let my daughter classify everything for you. Then you can look at a neatly typed list of contents and decide what should go to the Dorothy Killergallon museum and what should be…"

"Kilgallen," said Goldstein. "And there's not a museum. She was a very famous and very influential columnist. She was also a panelist on that TV show…"

"We don't care," said Mrs. Goldstein. "We don't care what television show she was on. Is she even still alive?"

"No," said Goldstein. He was beginning to get a little perturbed. "That's the thing. She died back in the sixties under mysterious circumstances. The police said it was suicide, but…"

"I still don't care," said Mrs. Goldstein. "Just have the shippers send it to Jhona. I'll call her and tell her what to do with it. OK? Can we go now? Please?"

As he was ushered out of the office for the last time, Goldstein took one last look at the old box. "Well, he thought. "At least I'll get a list of contents." Still it was like walking away from buried treasure. "What could be in there," he kept thinking. "It could be anything…"

IT COULD BE ANYTHING

Jhona Goldburg was Richard Goldstein's granddaughter, and pretty much the light of his life as the old saying goes. She'd spent much of her short life fostering grandpa's undying affections and generosity. Grandpa had always hoped Jhona would go into law and someday join his firm. But Jhona had other ideas. She actually wanted to save people—mostly from themselves. She was going to "go into" psychology, and she was going to do it in a nice liberal school as far away from the corrupted East Coast schools as she could get. The result – she was in her third year as a "Psych" major at UCSF, San Francisco's bastion of liberal brainwashing. At least that's the way Goldstein thought of it. "Good God," he said to his wife as she broke the news to him after a tearful encounter between the two women. "I guess her chances of meeting a nice Jewish boy are out the window, too."

Ah, the transgressions our young ones place upon our weary heads! Jhona's transition from safe, honorable conservatism into the dark, depths of liberal thinking was not the worst of the situation. Not by a long shot. No. The worst was an idiot whom she announced to a shocked family one spring break was her soul mate. *Soul mate!* His name was Peter Leaderson, and they were moving in together and would be building an honest life together, all without the phony, plastic values of the conservative right. It was left coast, baby, and there wasn't a thing anyone could do about it. So there!

The evening ended in tears and recriminations all around—a typical Jewish family gathering as far as Richard was concerned. And it all occurred without Peter having even the slightest clue about what was going on. It certainly didn't affect his appetite, that's for sure. He just kept on spearing latkes and slathering them with sour cream until Mrs. Goldstein wanted more than anything to spear *him* right through the ear. If they did manage to stay together for a long time, he would have to be introduced as Jhona's "special" friend.

Oy, she dreaded that. Think what the Meyers would say behind her back, that perfect, Jewish couple with the three perfect kids. The boys properly Bar Mitzvahed and their perfect, tall, beautiful daughter Bat Mitzvahed and holding onto a *doctor's* arm. And, worse, a wedding being planned to the T's for next June. She had to sit down with a thump on her Chintz armchair, as she couldn't get the awkward introduction out of her mind.

"Mrs. Meyer," her fantasy self said to the imaginary Mrs. Meyer, "I'd like you to (choke) meet Jhona's *special* friend. We all try to treat him as though he were, uh, normal."

In her mind's eye, Mrs. Goldstein could see Peter sloshing some red wine onto her white carpet as he vigorously pumped Mrs. Meyer's hand up and down. Of course Mrs. Meyer would look over at Mrs. Goldstein and say something like, "What a perfectly delightful boy. He's an ideal match for your Jhona." She felt a vicious migraine coming on.

Later that evening, Goldstein called his granddaughter. "Jhona, this is grandpa."

"Of course grandpa. I know. I'm just a little surprised to get a call from you. I know you hate talking on the phone. Usually it's grandma who calls."

"Oh, you know I love talking to you, Jhona. How are you?"

"I'm fine, Grandpa."

"How're your classes coming along?"

"Just fine, Grandpa."

"And how is your boyfriend, uh…"

"Peter, Grandpa. It's Peter, and he's fine, too."

"Good. Good. Listen, Jhona, I've got a little job for you. I'll pay you fifty dollars an hour."

"For what, grandpa?"

"Well, I have an old box from the firm. It's been sitting in storage for almost fifty years now. I need you to go through the contents and make up an inventory list of everything in the box."

"An old box? And you don't know what's in it? Is it important?"

"I don't know, Jhona. It could be. As an historical piece."

"Why would someone store it in your old office?"

"My partner received it from an old client way back in the sixties."

"Someone famous?"

"Yes. Exactly. A well-known journalist who was also on a popular TV show back in the fifties."

"Well, Grandpa, you had a lot of clients like that didn't you?"

"Yes, but this one was a bit special. She died under mysterious circumstances. The police said she committed suicide, but there were many unanswered questions. The box was sent to us for safekeeping, and I guess we all just forgot about it. Just like the world forgot about her."

"Are you going to tell me who she was?"

"Yes. Yes, of course. Her name was Dorothy Kilgallen. She was a very famous columnist, and she was on an old game show—as a panelist—called *What's My Line?*. It was very popular. The panelists would ask yes or no questions trying to guess the line of work the guest was in. She was the sharpest on the panel."

"Great. I'll Google her. Anything else? Anything about the mystery surrounding her death?"

"Well, what is most intriguing is that she got caught up in rumors about the Kennedy assassination. You know, the conspiracy theories. She said she had evidence that would, as she told some of her closest friends, blow the lid off of the whole case. She wasn't one to brag about things she didn't have. Then she suddenly died, so there could be something in the box… Or nothing. You never know."

"OK, grandpa. I'll get started as soon as the box arrives. Love you."|

"Love you, too, dear."

EXPECTATIONS

"Hey, Peter. Come here a minute," Jhona said.

"What do you want, Jhona? I'm almost on level three."

"I want you to come here. Put the damn game on hold and get in here. Jeeze. Do I have to beg you every time I need you to do something for me?"

"Alright. Alright. I'm coming." He muttered something Jhona couldn't quite make out. "God! He can be such a pain in the ass," she thought to herself.

"OK. Here I am," Peter said. "What is it that is so important?"

"Well, I just thought you might like to know that the house is on fire. Was that wrong to ask you to come in here to save my life? Should I have just left you in front of that goddamn television to burn up?"

"There's no fire! What the Hell are you talking about, woman?"

"Just think of it as a fire drill like the kind we used to have in school. The question is—could you get out in time? Do you know where to go? Will you be accounted for or tragically missing? Burned up in the flames that you could have avoided if you had just done one simple thing for your girlfriend, and that was to come here when I asked you to."

"OK. I'm here. There's no fire. What–do–you–want?" He would never understand women. Never!

"I just got off the phone with my grandpa. He's sending me a box, and he's hiring me to come up with a list of what's inside it."

"I'm not following you, Jhona. He's the one sending you the box. Why doesn't he know what's in it?"

"Because he found it when they were cleaning out his office. Remember? I told you grandpa was retiring and that they were closing it all up. He's sending all the files to the firm that bought them out."

"Yeah! So very, very interesting, Jhona. Now please tell me why, exactly, I should care."

"Can you stop being such a goddamn putz for just a moment and try, just for fun, try to listen to what I'm saying? OK?"

"I'm all ears, babe!" Peter said as he slid behind her and cupped her breasts.

"Stop that! Dammit! What the hell is wrong with you? This isn't about sex. *Listen* to me!"

"Oh, all right," said Peter. He dropped his hands, and Jhona twisted around so they were face-to-face.

"Look. Grandpa is paying me to inventory the contents of this old box, fifty dollars an hour. It's been sitting in his musty old office for almost fifty years. He wants to know what's in it, and grandma won't let him take the time to look himself."

"Fifty bucks an hour? That's sweet. It'll take you a long time, right?"

"No. It'll only take me as long as it will take me. I don't gouge my grandpa. He's given me stuff like this to do before."

"So, do you know anything about this mysterious box? Is it, like, some sort of treasure?"

"All I know is that it's from one of his famous clients. You remember, don't you, that grandpa represented many of New York's most famous people?"

"Oh, yeah. Of course, I do." Peter had only met the old guy once or twice when they were back in New York to visit Jhona's family. The old guy seemed nice enough, and Peter vaguely remembered that he was some sort of lawyer. He certainly asked Peter enough questions to validate that. But, in the end, Peter didn't really give him much thought. Jhona would ramble on about him occasionally—especially now that he was retiring. "So, what? Is the box from one of them?"

"Yes, the box is from one of them. What do you think?"

"OK. Am I supposed to guess now?"

"Look. All I want *you* to do is sign for the box when it arrives—in case I'm in class. That's all. Just sign for it. Don't open it. Don't start going through the contents. Nothing. Just sign for it, and bring it into the apartment and leave it there for me. Understand? Just sign."

"OK. Got it. Just sign. Who packed the box, anyway?"

"If you must know, it belonged to a woman named Dorothy Kilgallen. She was a famous writer and was on some TV show back in the fifties."

"Hey. Let's look her up on the Internet."

"No, let's *not* do that, *let's* not do anything except sign for the box when it comes. OK?"

"OK, babe! Now that we've got that taken care of, have you got a little time before your next class to, you know…"

The answer was predictable.

PETER, PETER, PUMPKIN EATER

If you were a casting agent for, say, an upcoming Broadway play all about typical twenty-something's, and you were looking for the lead role, Peter Leaderson would probably be exactly who you would cast in the part. At six foot-two, he had carefully practiced an "I don't give a damn about anything" slouch that was enhanced by his wardrobe. And that, without variance, was made up of jeans, a colored tee shirt usually stained by some recent meal, and an un-buttoned flannel shirt.

Nearly every sentence Peter mumbled, something that drove his girlfriend nuts, began with the word, dude. It was "Dude! Let's order in some pizza," or "Dude! Let's get high," or "Dude! Let's do it." The last statement directed to the long-suffering Jhona. Peter seemed to have a real knack for suggesting that they "do it" whenever Jhona was the least interested in doing anything with Peter. She was a serious student and parceled out her time. Something that only included "doing it" on weekends.

Not that she didn't like "doing it" with Peter, but he was constantly slobbering all over her, and if she gave into his ever-present urges, that's all they would ever do. It really made her wonder about where their relationship was heading. She also found it was nearly impossible to get Peter into a serious discussion about said relationship. It was always, "Dude! You know I love you. Doing it is just a big part of that love. That's all. It's part of my commitment to you, and to us, and our love. So let's do it."

She was really beginning to wonder if he was a shallow person.

Actually, if she really thought about it, it wasn't so much that Peter was shallow. He was actually a fairly bright young lad, it's just that he was, well, impulsive. Actually, that condition was pretty typical of boys his age. Yes, he was legally an adult, but still so racked with testosterone that it greatly affected his judgment, and impulses. Jhona was smart enough to know that he would begin settling down emotionally during the next ten years or so, and would probably be a very good and loving husband. Jhona had the benefit of being raised by a very sensible mother and taken enough great Psych classes to give her a mature, long-term view of her relationship. But, she had her limits, and Peter seemed to be adept at reaching them. He was going to take a lot of "training."

The situation wasn't helped much by Peter's adolescent fixation on his "bro-for-life," friend, Jeff Frankie. In Jhona's opinion, Jeff was a total moron who was actually quite skillful at bringing Peter down to his Neanderthal level. Jhona's plan for Peter was to gradually freeze out Jeff to a more reasonable level of interaction. Of course, Jhona was just a bit behind the power curve on the mysterious box. She forgot to warn Peter not to say anything about it to Jeff.

DUDE, HAVE I GOT SOME COOL NEWS FOR YOU

Jhona was right about one thing. Jeff's sense of humor was just slightly more mature than his heroes, the Three Stooges. Physical humor! That's where it was at for Jeff, the more physical the better. That included at times: setting someone's shoe on fire with a match stuck between the sole and the toe; goosing Peter at a formal event; eating mashed potatoes with his hands and pretending to sneeze; giving "wet Willies"; the list just goes on and on. In Jhona's plan to "maturize" Peter, it was the most perplexing element.

She couldn't just forbid Peter to see him any longer. That would be the best solution, but Jhona knew it wouldn't take. They'd been friends since age two, and Peter thought Jeff was "as funny as it's possible for a human being to be." There certainly wasn't any practical way to rehabilitate Jeff, that's for sure. Disapproving looks and snide comments could only be expected to do so much. She pondered this problem a lot these days.

She even conferred with her mother on the problem. Her mother wasn't much help. She just said that eventually Peter would outgrow all of his childish attachments and start acting more and more like a responsible man. Admittedly, his relationship with Jeff dragged him down into the morass of adolescence, but that was bound to fade over the next year or two. Once Jeff was in med school, everyone would see a big change—hopefully for the better.

In spite of Jeff's moronic sense of humor, he was actually a top student and currently working through a demanding pre-med curriculum at UCSF that just seemed to come easily to him. In fact it came so easily to Jeff that it provided him with far more free time than seemed natural. The guy never seemed to study. It was freaky. Jeff would sit in class outlining a lecture with his right hand while using his left to turn pages in a textbook, which it seems, he would be memorizing. When class let out, Jeff was free to annoy Jhona.

     Reflecting on what Jhona's mother said, Peter would point out that Jeff would settle down eventually. He would have to if he were going to become a doctor. And anyway, Jeff was applying to out of state med schools, so he only had about a year left in San Francisco. That thought helped a bit.

IT'S HERE! IT'S HERE!

It was late one Friday afternoon when the box arrived from the East Coast. Peter signed for it and then slid it into the apartment. Jhona wasn't home, and Peter had promised he that he would do nothing more than sign for it.

About five minutes after sliding the package into the middle of what served as their living room, the bell rang again. It was Jeff, so Peter buzzed him in right away. Peter himself was feeling buzzed just looking at it. He kept thinking that it had sat, forgotten, in Jhona's grandpa's musty old office for fifty years. It was like a time capsule. There could be anything inside.

Jeff barreled into the room in his normal fashion – more like he invaded the room than entered it. Striding into the living area, he just about fell on top of the package.

"What the hell… is this?" he said.

"Oh, it's a really cool package Jhona's grandpa sent her. It's…"

"A package! Dude! Let's open it."

"Oh, no!" Peter said. "I've got specific instructions to just sign for it and not to open it."

"Instructions! Do you even bother to listen to yourself? What? Does she have you completely trained? You're whipped, Dude. Totally whipped!"

"I'm not freakin whipped, Dude! I made a promise. How is that being whipped?"

"Well, why don't you at least open the crate? Surely your little darling couldn't object to that?"

"Don't piss me off, Dude!" Peter said as he began rummaging through the top kitchen drawer for a hammer or a screwdriver.

"Did you ever notice that every house has one kitchen drawer with all the junk in it they never need?" said Jeff. "No one can ever find anything they need there, but it's always the first place anyone looks. What, by the way, are you looking for, Dude?" He was running his fingers over the crate as though he would be able to know what was in it through "vibes" or something.

"Ow! Chesuts Fricking Cavrist!" said Peter. "Who the hell put an Exacto knife in here without the blade guard?"

"Hey, Dude, you're really bleeding. Where do you keep Band-Aids?"

"How the hell would I know? Jhona packs all that stuff away."

"Well, here. Let me get you a paper towel. Let me take a look at it."

"Careful, goddamn it. It hurts like…"

"Hey! I'm a pre-med student, and I say you'll be all right in a day or two. Just rinse it out real well and wrap that paper towel around it. Now, let's get that crate opened."

Peter was too distracted by his stabbing, as he was beginning to think of it, to notice Jeff finding a hammer. He found a small one (the kind a girl might purchase) and began whacking at the wooden frame, flaking off bits of wood chips.

"Hey, Jeff. This fricking thing really hurts. Can you imagine what it would be like to get, like, totally stabbed? You know, like with a shiv in jail, or something."

"Yeah, Dude. A total bummer," said Jeff. "This thing is nailed up like a coffin or something. Do you have any idea what's in it?" He kept banging at the frame.

"Would you please stop that, Jeff? I don't want to open it until Jhona gets home. Look. I've got a better idea. The box was from a dead chick that was famous back in the fifties and sixties. Let's see what we can find out about her on Wikipedia."

Jeff hit the box one more time. "OK, Dude. Fire up the tablet.

It didn't take long to dig up several articles about Dorothy and her mysterious death.

"Man! What a cool story, Peter. That box is from the chick's house?"

"That's right, Jeff. Jhona says the box was sent to her grandpa for safekeeping right after her death."

"Wow! Think of it. That box has been sitting there for nearly fifty years. Look, what about all this talk about her and the Kennedy assassination? It says she was going to blow the lid off the investigation," Jeff said.

"Yeah. Died before she could put anything together. I wonder what she had."

"And look, her death was a total mystery. It says she was the only person to get a private interview with Jack Ruby," said Jeff. "He's the guy who shot Oswald right in front of the police. That must have taken some nads."

"For sure, Dude! Why the hell would anyone do that? They had the guy captured."

"There's only two reasons I can think of," said Jeff. One, he really, really liked Kennedy and was, like, totally pissed that he got shot. Two, he was part of the conspiracy and wanted to keep Oswald from talking."

"Talking? About what?"

"About who else was involved. Look. Just do a search for JFK conspiracies. See? Look at how many books and articles came up."

"Yeah, Dude. There must be a hundred, and look at how many were written in just the last ten years."

"For sure, Dude. The last word on this mess has not been written."

"Hey! Maybe we'll write the last word," said Peter. What if the transcripts of that Ruby interview are right in this box?"

"Dude! That would be totally choice. Hellacool. We could be famous!"

PUTTING A DAMPER ON THINGS

Peter and Jeff kept chipping away at the wooden crate until they managed to expose the original cardboard box that had sat in the storage area for so many years. They cleared away the wooden scraps and swept up all the sawdust around the box.

"Hey, Dude. I've got a righteous idea!" Jeff said. Let's spark up a doobie and just, you know, absorb some of the vibes this box is definitely giving off.

The box certainly had a mysterious patina about it. It was hard for the two boys not to imagine themselves in a *Raiders* movie. Jeff noticed that the original packing tape had dried out and was lifting off the box.

He fingered it a bit and soon the whole seam became exposed. "Loook, Dude! You can see inside."

"Hey, Dude. No. I promised Jhona we'd only sign for it. No looking, man."

"Sure, sure, Dude. No looking. I got that. Buuuut she didn't say anything about peeking, did she?" said Jeff.

"You trying to get me killed? Do you even have a clue at how mad Jhona can get? She gets pissed for days if I don't fold her pants correctly out of the dryer."

"Oh, God! You are SO whipped, Dude. She gets pissed because you don't do her laundry right?" said Jeff. "May I make a suggestion? Why don't you just stick your head right into that sparkling clean oven over there and just end it all?"

"I can give you two reasons, asshole. Reason number one – that's an electric oven. I'd have to bake my head to death. Reason number two – there's no way I'm going to risk not being able to tap that super fine ass of hers."

"OK, good points both of them."

They were both laughing so hard and rolling around on the floor that they didn't hear Jhona's key in the door.

As the door swung open, Jhona just stood there taking in the scene for a moment. "Could one of you idiots help me with these groceries?" she said.

"Hey, Jhona," Peter said from the floor. "Look what came."

"Yes, I can see. And you opened it up even though I asked you not to," said Jhona.

"No, Jhona," said Jeff. "We just opened the packing crate. Look. We cleaned it all up just so you could start going through the contents right away. We haven't even looked inside yet."

"That's right, love," said Peter as he stood up and brushed himself off a bit. "We were waiting for you just as you said."

"Well, that certainly makes you my heroes for this afternoon anyway. Help me put these groceries away and then we'll have a look at what's in there. And put out that goddamn joint. You can't stay straight for more than five minutes at a time?"

After the groceries were put away, Jhona made some tea and brought three steaming cups over to the coffee table. She then went into the bedroom and came back with a yellow legal pad and a couple of pens.

"OK, before we get started, Peter, I want you to go downstairs by the dumpster and see if there are any clean boxes. If so, bring up three of them. What we are going to do is take out each object from this box and catalog it on this tablet after which we'll place the object into one of the clean boxes from the alley. OK?"

Both boys nodded, and, as directed, Jeff made his way downstairs. He returned in a few minutes with three clean boxes.

"Mrs. DoggieTail wanted to know if we are moving," said Peter.

"You mean Mrs. Dogsteil wanted to know if we are moving. It's Dogsteil, not DoggieTail. I hope in your stoned stupor that you didn't call her that. What did you say to her, exactly?"

"I don' know. Could of, I guess."

"Could of! Crap! I'll have to go down and apologize to her later. You're such an ass sometimes. You know she's ninety-three don't you? You think she's going to think you're funny with that Dogstail stuff? *Nobody* thinks that's funny." Jeff forced himself to stifle a chuckle as Jhona shot him a withering look.

Making a mental note to explain to Mrs. Dogsteil what a dork her boyfriend is, Jhona turned her attention to the box. She carefully opened the four flaps exposing the contents for the first time in half a century.

"Peter. Go get my phone. I think we'd better take a picture of each object as we remove it from the box," said Jhona.

"Cool," said Peter. "Just like opening up King Tut's tomb."

"Yeah. Just like that," said Jhona as she removed the first object.

TREASURE CHEST

The first item removed was a musty ledger about three inches thick. It was the very old kind with a cloth-bound cover with inch-high words that spelled out "Ledger." All of the entries were faded and had been made with an ink pen. It looked like the book chartered various expense items relating to the *What's My Line?* show. There were entries for wigs, limo rides, gowns and a host of other related items. Entries spanned a five-year period.

"Jeeze," Jeff said. "It smells like someone pissed all over it. Lookit that stain on the front."

This comment caused Peter to begin a convulsive laughter attack that had him back on the floor, grabbing his stomach and trying to get his breath back.

Jhona put the ledger to one side, took a picture of it and then made an entry in the yellow pad. There were six more ledgers and an odd assortment of tickets to a variety of Broadway shows including some to Dorothy's show, *What's My Line?*. They all dated back to the sixties and fifties. There were also some programs from various shows.

The programs had margin notes, probably from Dorothy. They looked like they had been made during a performance as notes for her column.

Next came five stacks of bound letters. Jhona was able to tell that most of them came from people who were well known during that era.

One of the stacks contained letters and other materials from people involved in the show. This stack included contracts for the show. There were several other stacks of papers, which proved to be contracts for a variety of other events.

"Jhona, look at these contracts," said Peter. "They've all got signatures from famous people—or at least from people who I guess were famous back then. I wonder if they're worth anything."

"What they're worth to me right now is exactly fifty dollars an hour," she said. "Please try to remember that none of this stuff belongs to us. OK?"

"Oh, I know, but those signatures could be the real treasure in this box," Peter said.

"As soon as we finish cataloging all this "treasure" as you put it, Grandpa will tell us what we can do with it – legally, that is."

"Hey!" said Jeff. "Ask him if we can sell this stuff if no one else wants it."

"Sure, Jeff," said Jhona. "I'll do that just as soon as we finish going through it. The exact minute we finish, OK?"

"You're just being cynical now," said Peter.

"Really? Cynical? Me?" she said.

"Yes. Really. You."

"I guess I was just born that way. So what in hell is this?"

"Oh, my god! It's a body part! I just knew we'd find one…" said Jeff.

It looked like the top of someone's head. Jhona gently took it out of the box.

"It's a wig," she said.

"Oh, gross!" said Jeff. "Who keeps a wig?"

"Get over yourself," said Jhona. "Actresses and people like Dorothy have to look good every day of the year, so most of them wear wigs. It's a lot easier than constantly having your hair done. I'll bet this cost a fortune. It looks like real human hair."

"Oh, that makes it even grosser," said Jeff.

Jhona ignored him and placed it on one of the piles.

"Let's take a break. I'll make some more tea. Do you guys want any?" Jhona said. She got up and walked into the tiny kitchenette.

"Tea?" said Jeff. "Don't you got no beer? That's what I could use."

"No. We're not drinking *no* beer while we're doing this. *Don't we got no beer!* Where did you learn English?"

"From the street, baby! I learned it from the street," Jeff said.

Jhona's electric kettle started making those shaking sounds as the water began to heat up.

"The only street you've ever been on is *Stupid Street*, and you probably got lost trying to find *Common Sense Boulevard*," said Jhona as she poured steaming water into her favorite cup. "If you idiots want some tea, the water's hot now, and you can pick out your own flavor – that is assuming you are both capable of dealing with scalding hot water—a debatable concept if there ever was one."

"Alright, let's all settle down. We've got a lot of stuff to go through yet," said Peter.

"Now you're starting to talk sense?" said Jhona. "I agree, I agree. Let's get back to it."

COME OUT, COME OUT, WHATEVER YOU ARE

The box had been packed in layers, which made it easier for Jhona to classify the contents. The next layer consisted of hundreds of black and white photographs, most of them featuring Dorothy in poses with well-known people.

"You know, Peter, your idea of selling autographs is not so bad. What if we paired the signatures with photographs of the same people?" said Jhona.

"Yesss, Jhona," Peter said. "We do a little work, and this box of dusty relics could really become a little treasure chest. And thank you for admitting that I had a good idea."

"I'm always willing to acknowledge a good idea," she said. "But that will only work if one of Dorothy's relatives doesn't want the box, and grandpa says we can keep it. We'll find that out after he has a chance to look over the manifest and contact any of Dorothy's descendants."

"How many of those are there?" said Peter.

"Well, she had three children according to grandpa. Each one of them probably had children, so there could be quite a group of them," said Jhona.

She sipped her tea and thought for a moment. "You know, I don't think we have to point out to them that they could make money off the contents. All we need to do is just list them accurately. Anyway it would be a lot of work—more work than most people are willing to do. I'll talk to grandpa about it."

There were just so many photos, and only a few of them had anything written on the back. The majority were very tiny prints, too, which made it difficult to identify the people in them. Most seemed to be taken at events with three or four people sitting next to Dorothy in one of those,

"Please scoot together for the photo and pretend you like each other" setups.

Jhona got up and brought back a large, plastic freezer bag and dumped all the photos into it. "We'll try to go through these later," she said.

Once the photographs were removed from the box, there was a piece of cardboard exactly the size of the box. It was kind of like a false bottom except that it didn't quite go all the way to the inside walls of the box, so something could be seen under it.

They carefully pulled up the cardboard sheet to reveal two matching tin cake pans. They fitted the bottom of the box perfectly. In fact, they could have been made expressly for the box except for the artwork on their tops, which advertised *Great Lakes Cakes* and had beautiful artwork depicting a highly decorated Indian standing on the shore of one of the lakes, presumably one of the great ones, looking off into the distance. Smoke from a campfire stately rose behind the Indian. He held a blanket over one arm as though he had just signaled something to an Indian out on the lake. Far off in the distance, just barely large enough to see, was a figure in a canoe; his friend, the other Indian?

"Dude!" Jeff said. "These could be worth something to a collector. They're in perfect shape. Look at how bright that illustration is. Like it was just bought yesterday."

Jhona gently lifted them out of the box. "Easy getting the tops off, Jhona. Don't scratch them," said Peter.

"You take them off, Peter," said Jhona. "You're better at that kind of thing than I am."

"Dude! I wish I had recorded that!" said Peter. "I'm better at something than you? Mind blowing, simply mind blowing."

"Dude!" said Jeff as he high-fived Peter.

"Knock it off, little boys," said Jhona. "Just open the boxes. Carefully."

Peter chose the box on the left and using his fingernails, gently pried up the lid. The box was filled with eight-millimeter filmstrips with different sized reels ranging from two to four inches.

"Wow," said Peter. "Would you look at this?"

"Yeah, maybe they're porno films," said Jeff. "Ancient porno flicks."

Jhona made a disapproving face and picked up one of the reels. She unrolled it past the leader and put the strip up to the lamp.

"Peter, do we have a magnifying glass?" she said.

Peter got one from the top drawer of their tiny desk and handed it to Jhona.

"Please, let it be porno. Please, let it be porno," said Jeff.

"Shut the hell up, Jeff," said Jhona as she squinted at the first few frames. "It looks like scenes from that old TV show she was on. That's all, just scenes with her sitting behind a cheap desk. Let me check some of the others."

"I don't think that's necessary, Jhona," said Peter. "Look. Most of these have dates marked on the leaders. The ones in boxes are labeled, too. They're all marked WML with a date. That probably stands for *What's My Line?*."

"No porno? Piss!" Said Jeff. "Let's see what's in the other box."

"Peter! How about washing your hands first," said Jhona. "They're disgusting. What have you been doing anyway?"

"Man stuff, honey," said Peter. "Man stuff."

Peter took all of two seconds to rinse off in the kitchen sink. "OK, let's see what we have in this box," he said.

Jeff began his chant again, "Porno, porno, porno."

The carefully lifted lid revealed little cardboard boxes of audiotape reels. There were some without boxes as well. They had a few inches of white leader. Some were marked, some not.

"Man," said Peter. "Ancient tape recordings. I don't even think we could find a machine to play them."

"That's for sure," said Jeff.

"Probably more interviews," said Jhona.

"Yes. Boring," said Peter. "Jhona, are you going to have to list every one of these *and* those films?"

"I'll check with grandpa tonight, but I think I'll probably be able to just list them as miscellaneous tapes and films," she said. "I guess I should check the labels, though, just in case."

Peter and Jeff got tired of sorting through the piles of old films and tapes that were beginning to surround Jhona. After a sneezing attack, Jeff signaled to Peter that they should go outside and smoke a joint.

"We're going to go outside and take in some fresh air," said Jeff. "This place is beginning to smell like my grandma's underwear drawer."

"Good. Go. Both of you."

It took the rest of the day, but by dinnertime, Jhona had typed up her manifest and emailed it to her grandfather. After dinner she decided the manifest couldn't be considered complete unless all of the films and tapes were listed as well. She sent her grandfather another email letting him know that an addendum to the list would be coming in another day. She knew her grandparents were still on their cruise and that grandma would never let her husband go through a long email until they got home.

Jhona checked her schedule and confirmed that the cruise wasn't due to dock until Friday. That gave her three full days to complete the project.

I GOTTA SOME-A-THING ESPECIAL FOR YOU

Sorting through all the filmstrips was more tedious than she thought it would be. At first she used her magnifying glass to look at the first few frames of each strip, but it was hard to tell what was really going on. After about twenty strips, she reverted to just copying down what was printed on the leaders. She felt the leaders were accurate enough for the purposes of an initial manifest. Each leader was dated and contained a title.

After a while it became clear that they were all films of the *What's My Line?* show. The tipoff was that each date on the leader was a Sunday, which is when the show was aired. Looking at the first few feet of film showed the *What's My Line?* logo for a few seconds, and then Dorothy would walk out from behind the curtains over to her desk where she was introduced and took her seat. The other panelists followed. *"What a tedious show,"* Jhona thought.

A closer look at the stack of films revealed that they had been placed in order, so Jhona was able to quickly list them all by referring to an online calendar from the years of 1950 through 1965. There were just over five hundred episodes in the box. They were all eight-millimeter prints, so they didn't have soundtracks. Jhona wondered if the box of audiotapes would provide the sound for each of the episodes.

As it turned out, each audiotape could be matched to a filmstrip. Without an old reel-to-reel tape recorder she had no way of listening to them to be sure. Plus, the tapes looked old and dried out. Some of them were flaking off pieces of the magnetic strip.

"Well," she thought, *"They probably won't be of any real value to anyone."*

She began carefully repacking the tin with the old, dusty tapes. Both the tapes and the films made an even stack that exactly filled the tin. She was almost finished when she noticed that the tin of tapes was full, but she still had one tape left over. She was sure she had packed them exactly as they had come out of the box, and there was no space left over for the extra tape.

She picked up the box and took it over to the reading lamp to examine it more closely.

"What's the matter?" Peter asked. Bored with the whole unpacking process, Peter had retreated to his favorite chair where he was reading the paper. Jeff had gone home to his dorm room.

"It's this tape. I, I, it won't fit back in the box."

"It won't fit back in the box? What are you talking about?"

"All the tapes fit exactly into the tin, but now there's this one left over."

"You must have packed them differently somehow."

"You think I packed them differently? Exactly how could that be? They all fit perfectly when I opened the box. They're like packing dominoes. They only fit one way. Look. See how perfectly packed they are? All except for this last one here."

"Jeeze, I don't know, Jhona. I didn't watch you pack them. Maybe you should start over. Just dump them out and start again."

"You're such a help. Whatever would I do without your magnificent help?"

"Let me see that one, Jhona. It looks different from the rest."

"How so?" Jhona asked as she passed the box containing the tape to Peter.

"Look, hon. The box looks brand new, and it's a slightly different color than the rest."

"Sure, but they all vary slightly in color."

"I know, but this one is very different. It's like brand new. No fading, no little tears or wrinkles."

"Can you read the writing on it? I couldn't make it out."

"Yeah," Peter brought the box under the light and squinted at the inscription. "I think it says, 'Quarter' or something. Let me have your glass."

Jhona wiped off the glass on her shirt and handed it to Peter.

"OK. That's much better. It's very faint, like the writing faded, but the box itself didn't."

"Can you read it?"

"Yes…I think so. It looks like it says *Quantum Tape*. Yes. That's it. *Quantum Tape*."

"Well that certainly clears everything up."

"You're being cynical again."

"You forget. I was born cynical. How about opening it up."

"Okay." Peter slid open the end flap and shook the tape out onto his palm. Unlike the other tapes which had small plastic reels, the tape in Peter's had was on a metal reel. Like the box it came in, the tape looked to be in perfect shape.

"Is there a leader?" asked Jhona.

"Looks like it," replied Peter.

He unrolled about a foot of white leader. There was an inscription which was about as faded as the box label.

"It says, *J. Ruby—1965*"

"J Ruby? As in Jack Ruby?" Jhona asked.

JACK WENT UP THE HILL AND JILL CAME TUMBLING AFTER

"Yes, yes," said Peter. "When I was looking up Dorothy on the Internet, I kept coming across this fact that she had been the only reporter who got a private interview with Jack Ruby. You remember he's the guy who shot Oswald, and Oswald is the guy who shot JFK."

"Right…so this could be the tape of that interview?"

"Yes. The notes of that interview were never found. She probably taped the interview and then put it away somewhere. Eventually it was shipped to your grandpa's office where it stayed in that storage room for fifty years. Now, you've found it, Jhona. *You've* found it."

"OK, but that still doesn't explain why it won't fit *back* into the box."

"Forget about that, Jhona. It's just some kind of fluke. We'll figure it out later. Now what we need to do is come up with some way to hear what's on this tape."

"Oh, no, buster. The first thing we do is find out what grandpa wants done with this box of goodies, and that includes the mystery tape."

"What a lot of effort for a box of junk that no one is going to want anyway."

"You don't know that. Anyway, grandpa has to chase down Dorothy's heirs and let them determine what to do with it. We'll just have to wait. I've sent the manifest to grandpa via email. His cruise is over on Friday, and he might need a week or two to get instructions from Dorothy's heirs. We just need to cool our heels for a couple of weeks."

"A couple of weeks? Look, Jhona. This is hot. This tape is a piece of history. Why can't we at least find out what's on the tape? You could add the results to your manifest as an addendum. I'm sure no one would object to that. How about it?"

"I don't know. This tape makes me nervous. It's just weird, and, I don't know…it's got a vibe or something. Look at how clean its box is compared to all the others."

"Jhona, let's just do one thing while we're waiting for your grandpa to get back to us. Let's just find an old reel-to-reel tape machine…"

"Alright, alright. Go find a machine somewhere. Meanwhile I'll think about it."

THE SOUL OF OLD MACHINES

Jhona didn't place the tape back in the cardboard box with the rest of Dorothy's mementos. Instead she shoved it under her side of the mattress. Since Peter seldom participated in household chores, and he never stripped or made the bed, she felt that it would be as safe from him as placing it in a bank deposit box, although, for some reason, she was tempted to do that instead.

That night she found it impossible to get any sleep. The tape kept entering her mind. She kept wondering what could be on it. It was actually spooky to her that the tape probably contained the voice of a murderer. Not only that, but arguably one of the most famous killers ever, and no one had heard what he had to say…except Dorothy nearly fifty years ago, Dorothy who had died not long after.

At one point during the long, dark hours, the reel seemed to float in front of Jhona's face. It slowly began turning, and the leader played out onto her bed.

She kept telling herself that she must be dreaming, but it all seemed too real. After a few seconds of watching the leader unroll, the tape itself began spilling across her chest. The reel kept unrolling, faster and faster. Soon she was completely covered by a huge pile of tape. There was much more tape on her then could possibly be contained in a small two-inch reel, but it kept unrolling and unrolling. The pile kept getting deeper and deeper, and Jhona couldn't move.

Jhona kept thinking she was awake. She could even feel the smooth, cold tape snaking across her face. It seemed to be probing, probing, looking for her mouth. As soon as Jhona realized this, she began screaming, but no sound came out except a gurgling. Her mouth was wide open in terror when suddenly she felt the tape reach her mouth and begin moving down her throat.

She was terrified. The tape made it hard to breathe…made it impossible to breathe. She was shaking, desperately trying to shake the mound of tape off her. *"Where was Peter? Why couldn't he sense what was happening?"*

Soon she couldn't breathe at all, and a cold darkness settled over her as she passed out.

AND A GOOD MORNING TO YOU, TOO.

Jhona was floating somewhere; perhaps in a lake, a warm lake. Her ears felt like they were underwater because there were no sounds…kind of like when you put your head underwater, that kind of quiet.

She wasn't cold, though…or wet. So she wasn't in water, but where was she? She was definitely floating. She opened her eyes. She was staring at the ceiling, but it was only, maybe, three inches from her face. She turned her head and looked down…at the bed. It was at least six feet below her. What was holding her up? Was she still dreaming?

Then a faint sound reached her ears and became louder, "Jhona. Hey, get up. Breakfast is almost ready, lazybones." It was Peter. Jhona began to descend. That was the only word for it. She descended kind of like a feather…swaying this way and that as she gradually lost altitude. It was crazy.

After about a minute she realized she was back on her bed. She could move. She moved her hands to her face and stared at them. Then she covered her face and began sobbing. It was a heartbreaking sound…the kind of sobbing only a woman can make.

She heard Peter's voice ascending the stairs, "Jhona. What's wrong?"

In a moment he was by her side. He gently removed her hands from her face and held them. His hands were warm and he had that smile on his face that made her hug him…every time she saw it.

She grabbed him and pulled him down onto the bed with her, on top of her.

"Hey, Jhona. What?"

She was hungry for him, more than ever before. She ripped open his bathrobe and pulled it down off his arms. Peter was totally confused.

Jhona had to have him, and now. She opened her nightshirt and placed his hands on her breasts. She was still sobbing. Peter felt his need rising. It seemed uncontrollable. He raised Jhona's nightgown over her head and threw it onto the floor. Then came her panties. Jhona was completely naked now, and wet. Unbelievably wet.

As Peter entered her, Jhona's sobs turned into deep, guttural sounds...like growls. Peter wasn't gentle. He felt like a wild animal taking his mate through the uncontrollable lust that consumed him. Consumed both of them. Soon they were growling, and Jhona was scratching, leaving deep, bleeding lines on Peter's back.

Their orgasms washed over them like lava from an angry volcano, and they both fell into a deep sleep...Peter still hard inside.

THE MORNING AFTER THE MORNING AFTER

They woke up about four hours later. Peter was still inside Jhona although he wasn't hard any longer. His penis hurt as he gently pulled it out, and Jhona stirred with a soft moan. Peter was afraid she might want to do it again. There was no way that was going to happen again. At least not for a day or two.

Jhona looked up at him with frightened eyes. "What am I hearing?" she said. There was a rapid knocking on the front door.

"Oh, man. It's probably Jeff," he said.

"What, what time is it?"

Peter glanced at the clock, "It's almost noon. I told Jeff to come by at noon. I'll get it."

"Good plan, but put on your pants first."

"Right. My pants. Hey. What was that all about this morning?"

"Just go. We'll talk about it later." Jhona felt a wave of fear wash over her.

As Peter moved down the stairs the smell of that morning's forgotten breakfast gave him a pang of hunger. He reached the front door shirtless and barefoot. He had definitely pulled something in his back causing him to wince with pain as he pulled open the door.

"Hey, Dude," Jeff said. "Aren't you even up yet? Why are you hunching over like that? Did you guys do it this morning? Man. You look like sex warmed over."

"Yea, well…sometimes a dude just has to…"

"Forget it. Where's the tape?"

"Hey, are you hungry? Want some breakfast? I've got some bacon and pancakes that just need to be warmed up. I'm starving myself."

"No, Dude. Had a burger on my way over."

"Well, I need to eat. Hey, wait for me in the kitchen. I've got to go ask Jhona something. Be right back."

Peter limped up the stairs holding onto the railing. Jhona was in the bathroom with the door closed.

"Hey, Jhona. Sweetheart. Are you OK? I have some pancakes and bacon downstairs. All I have to do is nuke it."

She answered him through the door. "I'll take a couple of pancakes, but throw away all that bacon. It's been out for hours. I'll be down in a minute." She didn't trust him with the bacon. For some moronic reason he thought once something was cooked it couldn't make you sick. Jeff was the same way. She guessed it was one of those guy things that were beyond the abilities of women to change or understand.

She was still trying to get over the shock of last night. The dream and levitation, that's what it was…levitation, had made her question her sanity. Wasn't levitation a sign of demonic possession? It just couldn't have been real. She *must* have been dreaming. As she thought about it while repairing her face in the mirror, the memory seemed to fade. The shock of it wore off enough that she became more certain that she had been dreaming.

That had to be it. She certainly wasn't choked to death by an audiotape. She woke up from that dream. Woke up to what? Floating three inches from the ceiling? That must have been part of the dream, too, but it seemed so connected to her awake state—she could even feel the floating descent. Those feelings were real—seemed real anyway.

Her face looked ten years older. There were actual bags and dark circles under her eyes, and she could swear there were several nasty looking wrinkles on her face that had not been there before.

That wasn't all. Her complexion had taken on a yellowish hue. It was hideous. She obviously had a lot of work to do before she could come downstairs for something to eat. The problem was…she was hungry, ravishingly hungsry.

VIBRATIONS

Jhona was going to tell Peter about the dreams, but she couldn't bring herself to do it in front of Jeff. He was always making fun of her, and she couldn't stand that this morning. One thing for sure, she wasn't going to sleep with that tape under her mattress again.

She pulled on a pair of comfortable jeans and a sweatshirt with UCSF stenciled on the front. She'd had it forever, and it was probably the most comfortable article of clothing she owned. It always made her feel better.

She decided to take the tape downstairs and find a place to hide it as far away from her bed as possible. She slipped her hand under the top mattress and began feeling around for the tape box. It didn't seem to be there.

She knew she hadn't moved it. It had to be there somewhere. She kept sliding her hand up and down the mattress until she got frustrated and began cussing. Cussing was one of Jhona's real skills. She knew enough cussing phrases to turn a sailor beet red. Her movements became more and more abrupt until finally, she just lifted up the mattress and flipped it completely over.

As it crashed against the dresser, it knocked everything off the top including her hand mirror and a crystal bowl that held some of her jewelry. The mirror and the bowl shattered when they hit the floor causing her to recoil from what she had done. It was a full-sized mattress. How could she have possibly flipped over something that heavy? She and Peter would flip it over about once every three months, and she always had to have help from him. There was no way she could have lifted it like that and sent it clear across the room.

As she was staring at her hands, she heard Peter coming fast up the stairs asking her what had happened.

Peter rounded the corner at the top of the stairs, but he was blocked from entering the room by the mattress.

"What's going on, Jhona? Are you OK? What the hell happened to the mattress? What did you do?"

Jeff followed up the stairs, his mouth wide open from the shock of seeing Jhona standing behind the upended mattress. "Holy crap, Jhona. What the hell…?"

Peter was moving under the mattress trying to get across the room to Jhona. "Jhona. Talk to me. What's going on?"

"I'll tell you what's going on. It's that goddamn, mother fucking tape. That cock sucking asshole fucking tape. That…"

Peter finally reached her and took her gently in his arms. She began to softly sob. "It's OK, Jhona. It's OK."

"Peter. Where is the tape?"

"The Ruby tape?"

"Yes, the Ruby tape. I put it under the mattress last night…oh Peter, I had the worst dream, and it seemed so real."

"A dream? About what?"

"Look, Peter. No tape. I put it under the mattress last night, and now it's gone. Did you take it?" She looked up at him very accusingly.

"It's downstairs, Jhona. I'm going to try to find a machine that can play it."

"You took it downstairs? You did?"

"No. I didn't take it. It was down there. Right where you left it. Right on top of the tin box with the rest of the tapes."

GET IN THERE AND STRAIGHTEN UP YOUR ROOM, YOUNG LADY

They had to put the mattress back on the bed just to be able to move around in the room. Jhona had slid down to sit on the floor while Peter and Jeff replaced the mattress and swept up the glass. They decided to make the bed later, given everything that had occurred.

After the bedroom was all put back together, they went downstairs, avoiding the tape box. Jeff and Jhona sat down at the cute chrome dinette table that Jhona had found in a neighborhood antique store. Peter heated up the pancakes and fried up some bacon from the package in the refrigerator.

Eating together made them feel much better…almost as though they were back in control of things.

"Peter," Jhona said. "There's something about that tape. Something bad. I don't know what it is, but I'm scared of it."

"What's there to be scared of, Jhona? It's just an old tape…an inanimate object."

"Sure, Peter, but it probably contains the voice of a killer. Ruby's voice."

"We won't know that for sure until we play it. I still think we need to hear what's on it as soon as possible.

"Peter, that dream, it wasn't just a dream. I woke up levitated. I was three inches from the ceiling looking right at it."

"You were what?"

"Three inches from the ceiling. Any closer to it, and my nose would have been touching it."

"Jhona. You must have been dreaming, or in some sort of a trance or something. That just has to be…"

"Peter. I was awake."

"Well, how did you get down?"

86

"How did I get down? I floated down like a feather. Gently."

"Like a feather, and you don't think you were asleep? Baby, I got total news for you. You were fast asleep, and I mean *fast*."

"Okay. Then explain the mattress. How did I flip it over by myself?"

"*Why* did you flip it over by yourself? That's more the question. *Why*?"

"I was pissed. Totally pissed and looking for the tape that I remember putting under it last night."

"At what? Pissed at what?"

"At being out of control. It was levitation, Peter. *Levitation*. Do you know what that's the first sign of?"

"Let me take a guess. Being totally out of your mind?"

"No. Not being totally out of my mind. Levitation is the first sign of demonic possession."

"What makes you so sure that's…"

"What makes me so sure that's what it means? Because I've watched tons of horror movies, and that's what it means. What else could it mean?"

"In the horror movies. That's what it means in the movies, but we're standing here in real life. Not in some movie."

"None-the-less, it happened, and that's what it means."

"Okay, Jhona. Okay. I just don't know what to say. Look, the library is probably open by now. Why don't Jeff and I take the tape over there and see if they have an old reel-to-reel recorder. We'll see what's on it and be back in an hour…two hours tops. Okay?"

Their apartment was on the corner of Filbert and Mason, so the North Beach Library was only about a block away over by the Joe DiMaggio tennis courts named after the famous baseball player who had lived in the city. At first Jhona didn't want to be left alone, but since they were taking the tape with them, she felt better about it. She made some tea and went out onto their little balcony to take in the sunshine and try to sort things out a bit.

The tea and sunshine calmed her down, but she was still troubled about the tape. There was just something weird about it. After a few minutes she went inside and dialed her grandfather's cell.

THAT'S WHAT *SHE* SAID

It was a clear, beautiful San Francisco day, and walking out their building's front door onto Filbert, Jeff and Peter both experienced a feeling of wellbeing and adventure. After all, anything could be on that tape.

Their walk to the library was short, but the bustling cars and people walking around made everything seem completely normal again.

"Dude," Jeff started in. "Your chick is totally bonkers. I mean way out in left field. What do you think is wrong with her?"

Walking San Francisco streets on a busy morning was a bit like running with the bulls at Pompano. You had to be alert and ready to dodge one of the fast little death machines that were carelessly wielded by asshole ad execs and stock brokers. For them, texting was far more important than watching out for pedestrians in crosswalks.

This morning proved to be no exception as a silver BMW blew through a red light just missing Peter. An angry blast from the jerkoff's horn jolted Peter out of his thoughts about Jhona. "Dude, let's talk about this when we get to the other side of the street," he told Jeff.

Jeff nodded his agreement, but neither of them said anything until they were standing at the entrance to the library.

When they got there, neither one could think of anything to say about the morning's events. In fact, the whole thing seemed unreal, like an intense dream that flakes apart and floats away after you wake up.

Jeff spoke up after a few long seconds of standing there. "Dude, the way I figure it is she was dreaming about the levitation thing, and pumping raw adrenaline through her system when she tipped the mattress. That's all."

"I suppose you are right. Let's just concentrate on finding out what's on this tape."

"Rave on, Dude. I'm right behind you."

WHISPER IN MY EAR

The morning had turned a bit to the cool side with a stiff breeze whipping up and scattering bits of paper along the sidewalk. The sun still had a bit more sky to climb to reach its zenith, but it provided a nice measure of warmth on their backs as they stood in front of the library door. They both knew this was their last chance to turn around, throw away the tape and walk away from the whole thing.

"Well, let's go in," Peter said as he held the door open.

"Dude," was all Jeff could come up with.

Unlike the main library over at the Civic Center, the North Beach branch was small and relatively quiet, making it a favorite place for all of them to come and study. There was something about the old brick walls surrounding the reading area that aided concentration. Actually, the whole building was made of brick, which was unusual for an earthquake city. The capper was that it was painted an ugly shade of orange. There were plans to tear it down and build a brand new building of course, but no progress had been made as yet. It was still standing.

There was always the background murmur of quiet conversation and pages being turned that was comforting to Peter. The reading area was located upstairs on a sort of half floor, which was open to the rest of the room below. The only problem was there weren't any secluded places where they could listen to the tape if they could locate a reel-to-reel tape machine.

Peter approached the main desk and stood in the checkout line behind an older Italian woman who was checking out a large stack of mystery books. She could have used one of the automatic scanners to check them out herself, but that wouldn't have provided her with the opportunity to chat with the librarian about her poor cat, Scamp. Seems the poor fellow had gotten out two nights ago and came home with three abscesses, which were going to cost her a pretty fortune, mind you, and she was on a fixed income since her dear husband, Charles, died six years ago and the social security had dried up.

The librarian just nodded sympathetically. He'd heard it all before.

When it was finally his turn, Peter held up the little box with the tape inside and asked him if there was a reel-to-reel tape recorder they could use to listen to the tape.

The librarian told Peter he was in luck. They had some old media equipment that was slated to be sold or given away when the construction on the new building finally started. He called over an assistant who looked like he never left the library. He looked vaguely familiar with a kind of permanent smirk. The librarian told him what to look for and instructed Peter to follow him. His nametag said "Ozzy."

Ozzy opened a little-used hollow door to reveal a dark, dusty room with cheap, metal shelving surrounding a small area filled with ancient media carts. Carl switched on a dim orange light and began moving the carts aside to make room for a scratched, rickety looking one in the back. On top of it was a wrinkled, dusty vinyl cover. After the cart was rolled into the cleared area, the assistant removed the cover to reveal an ancient Wollensak tape deck. It was dented and thoroughly scratched, but it looked like it had been made to survive many decades of hard use.

"Can you use this old soldier?" asked Ozzy.

"It looks perfect," Peter responded. "Where can we go to play our tape?"

"We don't have any private listening rooms, but I suppose you could just shut the door and play it in here." Ozzy looked like he was dying to know what was on the tape. He didn't make any moves to leave the room.

Jeff looked up from the tape recorder, "OK, thanks. We'll let you know if we need any help. Is there an outlet in here?"

Ozzy hesitated for about two heartbeats before pointing at one near the door. "Well, alrightie then. Just call if..."

"We will. We'll call if we need anything," said Jeff.

Ozzy did a one hundred and eighty degree pirouette and left the little room. He didn't close the door after himself.

Jeff closed the door making a face. "Well, let's git 'er done."

KILLERS HAVE FEELINGS, TOO

Peter felt a chill run up his back as he reached around and grabbed the tape from his back pocket. He shivered a little. Seeing that, Jeff just laughed. "Hey, what's the matter, Dude? Just do it."

"Yeah, yeah, I know, Dude. It's just that…"

"What? It's just that what?"

"Oh never mind." Peter removed the tape from the box and placed it on the spindle. He fished out the leader and ran it through the machine's pickups. Before loading it onto the take-up reel he took another look at the writing on it. "Dude. This is like, I don't know, monumental or something. I think we need to record this moment. Can you shoot a video on your phone when I turn it on?"

"Sure thing, dude." Jeff pulled out his phone and punched the video app. "Okay. All ready."

There was a hissing silence coming from the machine for about a minute. Then a female voice, "Jack Ruby. *Unintelligible*…nineteen sixty-five. *Unintelligible*…prison." More hissing.

Dorothy: "Mr. Ruby, first I want to thank you for granting this interview."

Ruby: "Sure, sweetheart. Happy to do it."

Dorothy: "First of all, I'd like to ask you why you've granted an interview to me when you've turned down so many others."

Ruby: "Well, they're all assholes, and you're not. You're cute."

Dorothy: "Cute?"

Ruby: "Sure, sweetheart. Cute. You're real cute."

Dorothy: "Okay…"

Ruby: "Look here, peaches cheeks, let's just get to the questions. They're not giving me much time, you know?"

Dorothy: "Okay, well I'd like to know…"

Ruby: "Yeah. Yeah, I know what you'd like to know. How big is my dick? Is that it?"

Dorothy: (Laughs) No, Mr. Ruby. I don't want to know that. I want to know..."

Ruby: "Sure, kid. I'm just messing with you, but you've got some nice tits. If you ever wanted to go into the stripping business, I could connect you with..."

Dorothy: "Please, Sir, as you said, we don't have much time, and I'd..."

Ruby: "Okay, sweet cheeks, Okay. I did it myself, all by myself. All right? I didn't have any help at all. No help."

Dorothy: "You acted totally alone then?"

Ruby: "Yes, totally alone. That's what having no help means. It means I got a gun, loaded it with bullets and went down to that goddamn basement and blew that fucking commie moron away. A total gut shot, too. Right in his little fucking pot belly."

Dorothy: "Can you tell me, uh, what your motive was?"

Ruby: "Now you're talking like a goddamn lawyer. Motive! He was a fucking commie. Loved that cock sucking Castro. He blew the president's brains out right in front of his wife, for God's sake. Isn't that enough motive for you? For anybody?"

Dorothy: "Are you evading the question? What made you take that action? Actually do it?"

Ruby: "Evading the question. No, I'm not evading the goddamn question."

Dorothy: "There must have been something else...some other motivating factor."

Ruby: "Oh, you're good, aren't you, really good. You want the truth? Is that what you're here for? The truth?"

Dorothy: "That's right. Go on, please. What drove you?"

Ruby: "I was possessed."

Dorothy: "Possessed? How, possessed?"

Ruby: "The only way someone can be possessed, by a demon. What the fuck else kind of possession is there?"

Dorothy: "You're sitting there trying to tell me that a demon made you do it?"

Ruby: "No. The goddamn demon did not *make* me do anything. He, or it, whatever, just possessed me. He, no it, crawled into my brain and kept, you know, talking to me. Well, it wasn't talking. *It* was me talking in my mind. You understand? Day and night. *Me* telling me that I had to do it for her."

Dorothy: "Her? Her who?"

Ruby: "I finally figured it out. I was her knight. The only one out of every other man in America willing to strike the very one who would destroy her."

Dorothy: "Destroy whom?"

Ruby: "The fucking grief would just kill her. To be dragged through a trial. It would go on and on. She would have to sit there in front of the entire world and testify about the horrors she saw. And then some smartass lawyer would probably get him off with, I don't know, five years with good behavior or something. Didn't you see on the TV where he was denying it? The little prick. There has to be punishment, retribution. It's the same for me. I'm going to die for what I did, but I'm a man, and I can take it."

Dorothy: "The she you mentioned? Are you talking about Jackie?"

Ruby: "Who the hell else? His head exploded. She had his fucking brains in her hands for God's sake. His *brains.* Can you imagine what that must have felt like? She was going to try to put them back, back into his ruined head. She had gathered them up and then she saw me. She started to crawl to me over the back of the car. She was trying to get to me. Her hands stretched out as best she could. I was there. Up on the hill. I was her knight.

"I started to run to her, but one of those secret service goons stopped her. Pushed her right back into that blood bath. I saw it in her eyes. The pleading. She was begging me to save her. *Heavy breathing.* "Then the cars all sped up and I couldn't make it… *Sobbing.* I tried, but…there was only one thing to do. And I did it, goddamn it. I did it."

Dorothy: "Well, you…you were on the hill? The grassy…"

Ruby: "She hasn't said a word about it. Not one fucking word, but I know she's grateful. I could see it in her eyes. Our eyes met you know. When she was on the trunk. Pleading with me. It hit me like a thunderclap. The demon or whatever it was made it so I could hear her. '*Do it,*' she was saying. '*Do it. Do it for me.*' She was screaming it, but I was the only one who could hear."

Dorothy: "Okay, Mr. Ruby. Would you like some water or something?"

Ruby: "Look, Dorothy. You're in danger, too. You must destroy this tape. If the demon gets to you…gets inside of you. There will be no other way…you'll have no choice…you'll have to ki…"

The tape ended. The only sound in the room was the end of it slapping gently against the pickups.

SEASON OF THE WITCH

Peter reached over to turn off the tape. The room fell into total silence, a kind of black, endless silence—the kind that happens after a tragedy. After all the bodies have been taken away and the streets swept up, the glass, casings and…the blood gone. They were both staring at the recorder. Peter re-threaded the tape and hit the rewind button.

After the tape had been rewound, Peter placed it back in the box. His first inclination was to return it to his back pocket, but instead he placed it on the table and looked at it for a minute.

"Demons?" Peter asked. "Demons? The dude thinks he was possessed by demons? What a crazy asshole."

"Yeah, well I guess it takes a lot of crazy to shoot some dude on live TV."

"More than that, Dude. You've got to be bat-shit crazy."

"He was that alright, Dude. He was totally that." Jeff had a look on his face like he was experiencing some digestive problems.

"Alright, Jeff, let's get back to Jhona."

Carl was waiting just outside the door. "Did everything work out for you?"

"Sure, Carl," Peter said. "The recorder worked just fine."

"Do you need anything else from us?"

"You mean do we need to check out some books or something? No, but thanks for asking."

Outside a cloud cover had whisked away some of the sun's warmth, and the noontime traffic was crowding the streets and sidewalks.

"Dude, look. It's lunchtime. Let's go over to Bocce's and get an outside table. I'll call Jhona and have her meet us there," Peter said.

The Bocce Café had what Jeff called *killer pasta* and featured a nice, covered outdoor eating area, which was perfect for cool days. They even had those outdoor heaters that would be fired up if it got too cold.

Over on Green Street, Bocce was a short walk from the library. They could even take Columbus, which slanted through the neighborhood making it an almost direct cut.

"We can play the video for her if it's not too crowded," Peter said.

"Yes. That was good thinking, Peter."

"What was?"

"To video it."

"Yeah, well I figured we needed some way to play it without having to find those old tape machines all the time."

"Dude? Do you think all that stuff about a demon could be, you know, true?"

"Jeff. Please. Demons? Really?"

"Well, I was just thinking about what happened to Jhona…all that weird stuff. Her dream and all."

"Sure, Jeff. A demon has to be the answer. Would you get hold of yourself? A demon? She was dreaming, Dude. Dreaming."

"But that stuff with the mattress…are you telling me that she's that strong?"

"Listen, my compadre, I would not be surprised at anything that chick does, and I mean anything."

A NICE LUNCH MAKES EVERYTHING BETTER

Jhona was glad the boys had gone without her to check out what was on the tape. It was weird, and it scared her a little. Well, more than a little. Actually, it scared the piss out of her.

After two cups of hot, soothing tea, she called her grandfather's cell. They were still on the cruise, so she had to leave a message. She told him that she had completed the manifest and had emailed it to him. In her opinion, there wasn't anything of real value, anything that is but the Ruby interview tape. For some reason she didn't mention the tape. She felt a little guilty about that, but she also felt that the fewer people who knew about it the better.

She asked him to get a determination of what to do with it all from Dorothy's descendants as soon as possible. She couldn't keep a slight bit of urgency out of her voice, but she didn't think her grandfather would pick up on it.

She was in the kitchen making a third cup of tea when her cell rang. It was Peter asking if she would meet them for lunch at Bocce. She didn't feel much like eating, but she did like the restaurant, and she was anxious to get out of the apartment if just for a little while.

Deep in the Italian section of San Francisco, Bocce Café was about as Italian as anything gets this side of Italy. Lavishly decorated with extensive garlands of garlic and flowers, heaping plates of pasta were served onto long tables, which created a family style atmosphere. The interior tables were always thick with the loud buzz of happy conversation and laughter. Peter always said it was one of the "good places" in the city, and they were lucky to live near it.

One of the covered outside areas was a bit more intimate with single, four-place tables, and was significantly quieter. Even so, it would have been very difficult if not nearly impossible to eat lunch there and be depressed. It seemed the perfect place to go at that moment, so Jhona didn't hesitate before grabbing a light jacket, locking the door and heading for the street.

Jhona headed east on Filbert until she reached Columbus and turned south. She passed Washington Square Park, her favorite place to hang out when the weather was warmer, and in another block turned left on Green Street. The café was another block up on Grant. The fresh air and mild breeze had helped clear her head, and she was feeling much more like a normal person.

The noon crowd was in full swing at the Bocce, and with the cool outside temperature, most of the patrons had chosen to be seated inside. Jhona made her way to the outside court with the smaller tables. As soon as she entered the room she spotted Peter and Jeff waving to her.

"Hi, guys. Did you find out what's on the tape?"

"We did indeed," Peter said as he stood up and gave Jhona a kiss.

"Well?" she asked.

"We don't have to tell you, Jhona. We recorded the session on Jeff's smart phone. Let's order first, and then we can play it for you."

They decided to split a plate of calamari and garlic bread with red wine all around. After they had finished that, they ordered ice cream for dessert.

"Okay, are you ready?" asked Peter.

"Ready as I'll ever be," said Jhona. The truth was…she was as scared as she was ready.

IF THE TRUTH BE TOLD

Even though there weren't many diners in the outside area, Peter thought it best if Jhona listened to the sound through ear buds…with all the cussing Ruby had done on the tape.

It had been a bit dark in the media room, so the image on the smart phone's screen was a bit indistinct. Peter and Jeff could hear the small chipmunk-like voice radiating from the ear buds.

Jeff was holding the smart phone, looking at the image on the screen. "Hey, Peter. What's that in the background there?"

"Where?"

"Look. See that monitor behind the tape deck?"

"Yes…what of it?"

"Keep looking. There. See it?"

"See what? I don't see anything."

"There it is again. A kind of shape."

"Where?"

"On the monitor. Behind the tape deck."

"Yeah. A kind of fuzzy shape moving around. It looks kind of like a Lava Lamp."

"What do you suppose that is?"

"I don't have a clue. We didn't have anything on in there except the tape deck."

"It must be some kind of magnetic interference or something."

"Yeah. Something like holding a magnet next to the screen."

Jhona took the ear buds out and looked at Peter. "What is this? I can't make anything out over that background stuff."

"Background stuff? What are you talking about, Jhona?" asked Peter.

"There's a sort of bass sound, like, I don't know, like a jacked up car stereo. Kind of a rolling, low frequency that blocks out what the other guy is saying."

"The other guy? Ruby, you mean?"

"I guess it's Ruby, but I couldn't make it out. Hey, look. What's going on with that monitor back there," Jhona pointed to the monitor.

"Yeah, we were just looking at that," Peter said as he put in one of the ear buds.

He could hear a heavy scraping sound. It was like someone taking the microphone and pushing it through a shag carpet. Peter noticed that the light in the monitor moved in concert with the sound. Then the video ended.

"Play it again, Jeff. You listen to it this time," said Peter.

Jeff hit the video icon again. This time there was not activity on the background monitor, and Jeff could hear Ruby perfectly. "I just hear Ruby, Dude, and look. There's nothing on that monitor this time."

"What the hell is going on, Dude?" asked Peter.

THE BEST POETRY DOESN'T RHYME

When they got back to Peter and Jhona's apartment, they weren't sure what their next steps should be. The answering machine's LED was showing a capitol 'E'. Jhona didn't know what that meant, but she hoped there would be a message from her grandfather.

She punched the *play* button. The first message was from her grandfather. He said he had heard from Dorothy's heirs, and they had no interest in the contents of the box. They made a request that the contents be destroyed.

The next message was from a male voice that sounded like it had been recorded by someone speaking into a long, metal pipe. Jhona couldn't make out what was being said.

The message after that one sounded the same, but had a different cadence making the words seem different than the first one, but Jhona couldn't understand them either.

She gave Peter a look and handed the phone to him as he walked over. There were nineteen messages, all of them just gibberish. The memory unit had been filled up with them.

"Peter, I'm getting scared. What in God's name is going on?"

"I asked that same question at the restaurant."

"Well, I don't know how, but I'm guessing it has something to do with that tape. Anyway, grandpa says we're supposed to destroy it and everything else in the box. Frankly, I'll be glad to get rid of all of it, but especially that tape."

"We've got to destroy all those photos and signatures, too?" Peter looked disappointed.

"Yes, everything. Grandpa's orders. We're not keeping anything, Peter. Especially not that weird tape, okay?" Jhona was as serious as she ever got.

"Well, before we get rid of the tape, I'd sure like to know what causes that image on the monitor in the background. What about that other noise on it? That grinding sound. Shouldn't we try to figure out what that is?" said Jeff.

"Yes, Jhona, that tape has major historical significance, even if all it does is prove Ruby was out of his gourd, which everyone assumes is the case anyway." Peter had that pleading look on his face. It never worked on Jhona.

"Peter," Jeff chimed in. "Look, I don't even remember there being a monitor in that room. Wouldn't we have noticed?"

"No, Jeff. Don't start with that. No monitor in the room? So, where did the image come from then?"

"Do you remember a monitor in the room?"

"No, but I was pretty hyped up to hear what was on the tape. I probably didn't notice a lot of things in that room. Plus, it was pretty dark even with the lights on."

"Any objection to watching the tape again?" Peter asked.

"How can we not?" said Jeff.

"Well, I for one want nothing to do with it," said Jhona. "You boys can watch it all you want. I'm going to take this box down to the dumpster. It stinks, and I'm sick of it. Not to mention that Grandpa wants me to confirm when it has all been destroyed."

"Okay, okay, Jhona," Peter said. "Do what you need to do, but leave the tape with us for a while…just until we figure out what the hell is going on. Grandpa didn't give you a deadline for when it all has to be trashed, did he? Would it hurt anything if we just delayed destroying the tape for a couple of days?"

"No way, Peter. This goddamn tape goes out with the rest of it." Jhona walked over to the box and threw the tape inside with the rest of the contents. Then she lifted it, but immediately put it down. This thing is too heavy, Peter. I'm going to need your help."

"Before we get started with that there's something I think we really need to do."

"What's that, Peter," Jeff asked.

"We need to archive this video. Give me a minute so I can move a copy of it to our cloud account."

"You've got a cloud account?" asked Jeff.

"Yes, we back up all our school papers and tax forms, that kind of stuff. There. Done now."

Peter got up from the kitchen table and walked over to the box. "We'll be right back, Jeff."

"No. I'll help." Jeff walked over to the box and picked up one end.

"Wait a minute," said Peter. "I've got to put on my shoes."

"Okay, Peter, but I sure hate to trash all those photos and signatures. Jhona, isn't there any way…"

Jhona just gave Jeff a look.

They picked up the box and with Peter leading the way, walking backwards, they disappeared through the door. Jhona could hear them treading down the stairs. She looked out the bedroom window down at the alley. She saw them emerge from the back door and upend the box into the dumpster.

"Too bad, Dorothy. That pretty much ends your story," Jhona said to herself. *"Well, we've still got this video. That'll be easy to get rid of. All we have to do is erase it."*

Jhona picked up Peter's phone and hit the video app. She selected the file marked, *Ruby*. She was about to erase it when it suddenly started playing. Jhona could see the monitor in the background. There was a shimmering shape on it kind of like a Lava Lamp. It was like a silver blob moving back and forth.

She heard Dorothy's voice. "Mr. Ruby first I want to thank you…"

Then a kind of grinding sound drowned Dorothy out. It seemed like words as if they had been made by using the noise a coffee grinder makes. She could just make out what sounded like a word or two. It sounded like her name. Just barely. "Jhona, Jhona, Jhona…" it kept repeating, but it was saying Jhona. There was no doubt of that at all.

It was hypnotic, and the words were in time to the swaying of the blob on the monitor. Unconsciously, Jhona began swaying side-to-side with the blob. Side-to-side. Back and forth. A tiny bit of spittle dropped from her mouth onto the table. Then there was more spittle. It formed a puddle on the table. Jhona dropped her face right into it. "JHONA," the voice said clearly and distinctly. The teakettle Jhona had set on the stove began screaming.

"JHONA. JHONA. JHONA." Jhona soiled her pants.

HEY DUDE

While they were climbing back up the stairs, Peter stopped and looked at Jeff. "You know what we need to do, don't you?"

"No. What?"

"We need to go back into that room and take some pictures of everything inside it."

"To see if there really was a monitor?"

"Yes. It still bugs me that I didn't notice something like that."

When they opened the apartment door, both of them recoiled from the thick smoke that rolled out onto the hallway. Peter screamed, "Fire!" and ran into the apartment keeping as low to the ground as he could.

He was choking and coughing, but the worst thing was that he was disoriented and he couldn't spot Jhona. He started yelling for her, but each breath caused his throat to burn and made him cough even more.

Finally, he began crawling across the floor until his hand touched a metal leg of one of the chrome chairs. It was turned over on its side, and just next to it, he felt hair. It had to be Jhona.

Peter grabbed a handful of what felt like her collar and began moving back to where he hoped the door was located. She was heavy and not moving. Peter was on the very edge of panic, and he heard someone screaming, "Jhona. Jhona." He realized the screams were coming from him, and he began uncontrollably coughing again. His eyes were burning so badly that he had to close them. He felt his grip on Jhona slipping. Then he couldn't hear or feel anything.

Way back in his mind something was forming. It was like he was sitting in a dark theater with the fire being like a movie playing on a big screen. There was something moving in the rows behind him, but he couldn't turn and look at it. None-the-less, it was there. Something as black as the theatre itself, but something strong and growing stronger. There was laughter, too. Not humorous laughter. Menacing laughter.

Then he heard someone or something talking. He could just make out the words. Just barely.

"Mr. Ruby first I want to thank you..."
"Mr. Ruby first I want to thank you..."
"Mr. Ruby first I want to thank you..."
"Mr. Ruby first I want to thank you..."
"Mr. Ruby first I want to thank you..."
"Mr. Ruby first I want to thank you..."
"Mr. Ruby first I want to thank you..."
"Mr. Ruby first I want to thank you..."
"Mr. Ruby first I want to thank you..."
"Mr. Ruby first I want to thank you..."
"Mr. Ruby first I want to thank you..."
"Mr. Ruby first I want to thank you..."
"Mr. Ruby first I want to thank you..."

* * * *

He felt himself being lifted. Six arms linked together under his body by holding hands, three on one side and three on the other; like pallbearers. Then there was a softness, and the feeling of straps, and then a rolling sensation. It hurt, but he was able to open his eyes. He was looking at the inside roof of an ambulance when a stranger's face entered his field of vision.

"You'll be OK, son. You just inhaled a lot of smoke." The face was chubby with a patch of rosaceous marking the chin, which flapped around a bit as the guy talked. When he was finished, the face broke into a broad smile that reminded Peter of the Cheshire cat. Peter expected the rest of the face to fade leaving only the smile, but it didn't.

He wanted to ask about Jhona, so he tried talking, but there was something on his face, an oxygen mask, of course. He could hear the quiet hiss of the gas being pumped into his nose and mouth. It felt cold. Then the face disappeared from his field of vision.

Peter closed his eyes and tried to concentrate on what the voices were saying outside the ambulance. It was Jeff. He was answering questions being put to him by someone with a deep voice. They were saying something about the girl. No burns. Treatment for smoke inhalation. Did she have asthma? Couple of days in the hospital. Lucky. The guy's OK, too. He'll get checked out at the ER. Lots of smoke damage. Weeks before they can move back in. Teakettle started the fire. Left on the stove. Couldn't figure out why. The girl was sitting right there in the kitchen. Curious, that.

Then the attendant shut the back door and sat down in one of the jump seats next to Peter's gurney. Peter could hear both doors in front closing, and the ambulance began moving.

I'LL TAKE THE HIGH ROAD, AND YOU
TAKE THE LOW ROAD

After he was discharged from the ER, the next thing was to visit Jhona. Jeff wanted to come along, but Peter said no. The one thing Jeff did talk Peter into was to let him go down to the dumpster and retrieve the tape. There were just too many weird things about it to just sit back and let it be carted away. Luckily trash pickup wasn't scheduled for three more days.

Later that evening, Jeff told Peter that while Peter was in the ER, he went back to the library to have a look at the AV storage area just to see if there was a monitor in there or not. He said the librarian behind the desk was a different "dude" than when they went in. The guy also said that he didn't know which library aid Jeff was talking about. Furthermore the dude claimed he had been behind the desk when they supposedly made their visit.

What was really weird was that the dude said there wasn't an AV storage area like the one Jeff described, and that they had gotten rid of all the tape recorders and other obsolete items years ago. Totally "freaked" by this news, Jeff had led the guy to where the storage door had been. There was only a brick wall. The librarian dude said that the only thing behind those bricks was the alley out back.

As freaky as all that was, Jeff said that they still had a really good option to continue this investigation. He said he knew a guy in the Physics Department at USF who might be able to analyze some of the weird noises on the tape. Jeff was sure the guy would have a reel-to-reel machine.

"You should see this guy, Dude. His name is Joe Crullmar, Doctor Crullmar. He collects audio/visual equipment, because he's really into recorded sound. Every time the AV department upgrades their machines, they give the old ones to Joe. He's got every old AV machine the department ever purchased. Once he even showed me an actual wire recorder. He told me they were used right after the war before audiotape machines were available.

"You might not believe this, but he told me that these early tape recorders were invented by the Germans during World War II, and there was a special contingent of soldiers sent to Germany right after hostilities ceased. Their mission was to capture wire and tape recorders, which they did, and he has one of them in his collection."

"How did you get to know him?"

"Dude, I took his course in quantum physics. It was an elective for me, and it turned out to be one of my best classes."

"Do you think we should play the tape for him?"

"Oh, Dude, absolutely. The other cool thing about him is that he is totally into paranormal stuff."

"What paranormal stuff?"

"He integrates quantum theories into paranormal theories."

"I don't think I understand. He does what again? What has paranormal have to do with all this?"

"We can get into that later, but what triggered the whole thing for me was that we needed to find another tape recorder. I want to listen to that tape again."

"So, we trade a spooky library guy for a kooky physics professor?"

"Well, that's just the thing. We don't just need a tape recorder to hear the tape again, but, Dude, this is the part that's so cool. He's into white noise."

"What the fuck are you talking about, Dude? When did I ever say anything about white noise?"

"Dude, you don't get it," Jeff's knee started moving back and forth. "White noise is something that can appear on a recording, like at a gravesite. It's ghosts, Dude, ghosts."

"White noise? Ghosts? Are you referring to that movie with, who was in it? Kevin Costner or someone?"

"Yes, the movie, the first one, though, not the second one. It had Michael Keaton in it. That's what I'm talking about."

"Dude, I still don't get you. You mean this professor of yours is into white noise or something?"

"You got it, Dude. Doctor Crullmar is a leading researcher in white noise, or what he calls, electronic voice phenomena. EVP."

"Just like the movie."

"Yes. Exactly like the movie."

"So what does he do?"

"Well, he takes some of his recording devices to places where people have seen ghosts, you know, haunted houses, graveyards, that kind of thing."

"So we're going on a ghost hunt now?"

"Could be, Dude. Could be. I'm talking about that grinding sound."

"So he would, what, process that grinding sound to see if a ghost was on the tape?"

"Well, maybe. If he thought it was something like that. I mean, look at all the weird things that have been happening, Dude. Something creepy is going on."

"Well, OK. Make an appointment with him, but I've got to go visit Jhona first."

I NEED SOMEBODY

Jhona had inhaled a lot of smoke, so her doctor decided to keep her in the hospital for a couple of days. "For observation" he said. It didn't look like anyone was doing much "observing" when Peter went to see her during visiting hours later that evening. The nurses were all gathered around their little "station," and talking. It took him awhile to get their attention long enough to ask what room she was in.

Flowers in hand, Peter gently knocked on her door, and a weak voice said, "Come in." Jhona was inside an oxygen tent thumbing through a copy of *Woman's Day* magazine. She smiled when she saw Peter.

"How are you doing, champ?" Peter asked.

"I'll be OK as soon as I get all the smoke out of my system. The doctor said it triggered some asthma, which I didn't even know I had. I didn't suffer any real injuries, which is a minor miracle."

"Well, thank God for that."

"Oh, yeah, before I forget, thanks for saving my life back there. I'll bake you a cake or something when I get out of here."

"Hey. No sweat."

"So what's with our apartment?"

"Mostly smoke damage. A lot of our things smell like smoke—especially our books. The stove will have to be replaced and the whole place repainted. The landlord says it will take about two weeks. He wasn't real happy to hear that the fire started because you left a teakettle on the stove too long, but there was a question about sub-standard wiring, so he shut up about it.

"I'll stay with Jeff until you get discharged, and then we'll have to come up with a plan B."

"Peter, really weird things are happening to me since we found that tape. I told you about the levitation…"

"You mean the levitation dream."

"You go on thinking it was a dream if you like, but I was the person it was happening to, and I guarantee it wasn't a dream. Then there's the fire. I was getting ready to erase that video when I fell into a kind of ugly trance. The next thing I knew, I was here."

"Well, erasing the video from my phone wouldn't have gotten rid of it. I uploaded it to our cloud service for safe keeping."

"Safe keeping? You want to keep it safe? From what? How about me? Don't you want to keep *me* safe, because I think I'm in all kinds of danger here. I was almost burned alive. Remember?"

Jhona began coughing.

"Easy, Jhona. Easy. We just need to find out what's going on. That's all."

"When you get back to Jeff's apartment, would you please call my parents and tell them I'm alright? Tell them not to worry, and that they don't need to fly out here. That's all I need, my mother out here."

GEEKS RULE

Joe Crullmar. Peter was expecting one of those skinny, pale guys with a prominent Adam's apple that bounce up and down when they talk. Guys who are *interested* in things, all kinds of things except football strategy and those ever mysterious creatures known as women. Joe was everything but.

A self-described "gym rat," Joe featured a well-toned, muscular body that rose a full six-feet-six inches off the surface of God's green earth. He was a very dark-skinned black man with a 70's style solid grey Afro that capped his head like a halo and shone like polished steel wool. But the most impressive feature was his broad, infectious smile. Greeted with that smile and a bone-crushing handshake, Peter didn't know what to think.

"Welcome to USF's vaunted physics department. Peter, Jeff tells me you have a fifty-year-old audio tape that you'd like me to analyze."

"Yes sir."

"What can you tell me about the tape?"

"What do you want to know?"

"Well, who made it, where you got it, and why you want me to listen to it?"

"Okay. It was made by an investigative reporter named Dorothy Kilgallen."

"Dorothy Kilgallen? The TV panelist for "What's My Line?"

"Yes sir. She was also an investigative reporter, and she managed to conduct the very last interview with Jack Ruby, the..."

"The guy who shot Oswald?"

"That's right, sir. Anyway this tape is the recording Dorothy made during that interview."

"Does anyone else know...I mean where did you get...?"

"It was in a box of Dorothy's private papers that my girlfriend's grandfather was storing in his law offices in New York."

"How did you obtain it?"

Peter was beginning to feel a bit uncomfortable. "My girlfriend, Jhona is her name. Jhona's grandfather was closing down his law office and asked her to inventory the contents of the box. He had been Dorothy's attorney."

"And you found the tape in the box? Did you listen to it?"

"Well, yes. We did. But that's when all the weird stuff started happening."

"Weird stuff. Maybe you should just go through the whole story from start to finish, and I won't interrupt until you're done."

With that, Peter described all of the events leading up to their visit with Doctor Crullmar.

"So, you can see, Doctor Crullmar, we are baffled, and Jeff, here, thought you might be able to help us figure out what's going on."

"The most I can do is analyze what is on the tape and maybe come up with a theory as to why 'whatever it is' is going on. I assume you have the tape with you. May I take a look at it?"

Peter carefully pulled the box out of his backpack and handed it to Crullmar. The doctor turned the box over and over and then picked up a magnifying loupe. He carefully examined every surface of the box and then looked up.

"You say this tape is over fifty years old?"

"That's right," Peter nodded.

"I think you are right about the weirdness. It starts with this box. There is absolutely no sign of age; no discoloration of the fibers. The ink is bright with no fading. It doesn't even have a musty smell. It was in a box filled with papers?"

"Yes, it was, and the box had a very musty smell. It sat in the back of an old storage room for fifty years."

"That's curious that it wouldn't pick up any of the smell. Did the whole room have a smell like that?"

"We don't know. All we got was the box it came in, and it really smelled."

"The tape was inside a tin box filled with other tapes. That box was at the bottom of the bigger box under a piece of cardboard that was kind of like a false bottom."

"Well, that could have protected the tape somewhat, anyway. What were the conditions of the other tapes?"

"I don't really remember, but I think they looked old. This one stood out because it looked newer than the others."

"OK, so we can assume that Dorothy bought a new tape just for the interview, and somehow it was protected from out gassing and the other factors that cause aging. Let's take a look at the condition of the tape itself."

"Sir, what is out gassing?" asked Jeff.

"Nearly every manufactured product has various gasses that are slowly released over time. This is especially true with paper goods and, I would imagine, Mylar tape products like this. The gasses are slowly dissipated from the product over a surprisingly long time. That's where a lot of the musty smell in your box came from.

Crullmar put on a pair of white, cotton gloves and gently removed the reel.

"Gloves. Great idea. Wish we'd thought of that," said Jeff.

Crullmar unwound the first two feet of leader and tape.

"Look at how the writing on the leader has faded. The rest of the tape looks brand new. That's curious. There's no flaking, scoring or chipping. It looks like brand new tape.

"Shall we give it a listen?"

"Wait, doctor. Before we do that, Jeff and I would like you to take a look at a video we made when we first played the tape."

"You found another tape machine?"

"Yes, at the North Beach Library. It's right around the corner from us. The tape is really weird, and what's more when we went back to the room we were in…with the old recorder? It wasn't there."

"Wasn't there?"

"That's right. Gone. Just a wall, a brick wall. No storage area, no tape recorder. Nothing. Even the two library people who helped us were gone. The two people working there had never heard of them."

"Well, that's a mystery for sure. Anything else happen?"

"Quite a few things, Doctor. My girlfriend swears that she was levitated when she was taking a nap, and then there was the fire…"

"Fire? That's not good. Where was the fire?"

"In our apartment. Jhona put on some tea, and then, kind of blanked out, and the stove caught fire. She's still in the hospital from smoke inhalation"

"Let's take a look at your video."

Jeff pulled out his phone and opened his cloud account. It took him a minute to find the correct file and download it.

"Okay, Doctor," Jeff said. "It's really weird, but there is a monitor in the background in the video that wasn't in the room. You'll see it."

The video began. The monitor in the background started flickering. Dorothy's voice could clearly be heard. *"Mr. Ruby, first I want to thank you…"*

Then the monitor in the background began pulsing to the rhythm of the voice coming from the recorder. As soon as it was perfectly aligned Ruby's image appeared on the monitor screen. It started saying, *"You disappoint me,*

Doctor Crullmar. You really do. You disappoint me, You disappoint me, You disappoint me, You disappoint me, You disappoint me, You disappoint me, You disappoint me, You disappoint me, You disappoint me, You disappoint me, You disappoint me."

The voice reached a fever's pitch and then the tape ended.

IF YOU'D LIKE TO MAKE A CALL...

Jhona was getting sick of just sitting in that stupid oxygen tent reading inane women's magazines. Surely today's women cared about more than *How to Decorate a Table that will be the Envy of all your Friends*, or *Ten Sex Secrets that will get your Husband off the Couch and into the Bedroom*.

The sad thing was that at some level, she was actually a little interested in both subjects. Not that she really had much of a problem with the second one. She could get Peter off the couch and into the bedroom all right. It was getting him off the couch to take out the garbage that was the problem. None of the magazines had any suggestions for accomplishing that.

Completely bored, she turned her hands over and began a critical assessment of her nails. They were starting to look really, really bad. They'd grown out since her last manicure, and her habit of picking them when she was stressed hadn't helped the situation much either. She needed them done, and she needed them done soon.

The funny thing was...as she looked at them, they would get fuzzy and indistinct. If she moved them from side to side, they would become nearly invisible until she stopped them. Then they would become clear again. Move them...fuzzy. Stop them...clear. Was there something wrong with her vision?

It was probably some sort of effect caused by inhaling all that smoke. Should she mention it to the doctor, she wondered? Just as she was thinking that over, the "thing" stopped happening. She decided not to say anything, but decided she had to get out of here.

And soon.

DID SOMEONE LEAVE THE CAKE OUT IN THE RAIN?

Both Peter and Jeff were totally freaked by the video. "What in holy hell was that?" Jeff blurted out.

"Dude! The voice was talking to you, Doctor Crullmar. Did you hear that?" Peter was beginning to feel actual fear. His hands started shaking.

Doctor Crullmar was less affected by it. "Look, lads. I've seen enough of this kind of thing happen. We're just being subjected to a kind of possession. Not a possession like in the movies where a demon is taking over our bodies. It's different than that. Let's hear what's on the actual tape."

Crullmar walked past a twin stack of papers and folders into a small room in the back. After some crashing sounds and a few grunts from the doctor, he emerged wheeling an ancient, black media cart holding a bulbous-looking tape recorder.

"This is my vintage Grundig." He seemed pleased with himself. "It's a circa nineteen fifty one model that was only used by a little old lady to record sermons at her church. Seriously." He was actually beaming.

"Anyway, it's in perfect shape, but we're not going to use it merely to listen to your tape, we're going to make a digital copy of the contents. It'll be a bit like the video you made of the tape that we just listened to, but much more sophisticated."

Cullmar unrolled a patch cable that was sitting on one of the lower shelves of the media cart and plugged it into a female output jack on the recorder. He then plugged the other end into the laptop computer sitting on his desk and turned the computer around so the boys could see the screen.

"Okay boys, what we're going to do is feed the audio from the tape directly into a voice editing program that I have on my laptop. We'll then be able to look at all the sounds on the tape and isolate them. After that, we'll be able to manipulate them. By that I mean speed them up, or slow them down, or even adjust the volume of specific sounds.

"However, before we get started, I need to explain what we are doing not just how we are doing it.

"What I believe is happening here with your tape and your video recording is that you are picking up what we call electronic voice phenomena. It's how ghost hunters record "voices" of the departed."

"You're telling us that you are a ghost hunter?" said Jeff.

"No, I don't go out to capture EVPs. All I do is help people analyze what *they* have captured. I have no personal desire to communicate with the departed. I help analyze these recordings as part of experimental evidence that can help prove a physics theory of mine.

"It has to do with Quantum Physics. Are you two familiar at all with Quantum and Newtonian/Relativity Physics?"

Both boys looked at each other, and then Jeff spoke up, "All I know is that in Quantum Physics everything is uncertain."

Crullmar chuckled at that. "Pretty good, Jeff. That's actually quite accurate. Quantum Physics and Newtonian/Relativity Physics are quite different, and yet they both describe the real world. Newtonian accurately describes our everyday world including the vastness of the universe. Everything in that side moves along in a predictable manner. Gravity holds galaxies together and all the stars and their planets move around each other in totally predictable ways. Relativity sets the speed of light as the fastest anything can move and sets forth the principal of the space-time continuum. Essentially, that means time is our fourth dimension and is bound to space.

"If you look at our moon, for example, you can accurately calculate where it is right now, and based upon its velocity relative to the earth, where it will be in a day, or in any other measurement of time. In other words we know where everything is right now and where it will be as time goes by.

"Would you two like something to drink before we get into the Quantum world?"

"Yeah," said Jeff. "Have you got anything alcoholic?"

Crullmar chuckled and tossed them a couple of bottled waters from his small refrigerator.

"Now, we take a look at the infinitely small part of our universe, the smallest particles that make up neutrons, electrons, and atoms, but way, way smaller than those even; basically, everything smaller than an electron. What we find is that energy particles, like light for example, are both particles and waves. Which one depends upon how you measure it. If you measure it as a particle, it will act like a particle. If you measure it as a wave, it will act like a wave.

"The point is that in the very small world of elemental particles, when you look at something, you change it. Which means that you can't measure anything in the Quantum world without altering it. Observation becomes part of the process.

"The key thing to remember is that if you *can* locate a particle, you *can't* know where it is going. If you calculate where a particle is going, you *won't* be able to see it.

"The really freaky thing about the Quantum world is that an object may be in two opposite states at the same time. Schrodinger's famous thought experiment stated that if you have a Quantum cat in a box, it is not either dead or alive, but in both states at the same time."

"Sure, Schrodinger's cat. We studied that in your physics class," said Jeff. "But what does all this have to do with our tape?"

"The point is that all this Quantum stuff is real, and all the Newtonian stuff is real. It's just that Quantum physics only operates in the sub-particle part of the universe while Newtonian physics only describes the rest of the universe. Up until recently, it was thought that these two rules of physics never met, but comfortably separated by the relative size of things. Very small things: Quantum physics. Very large things: Newtonian physics."

"You said up until recently?" asked Jeff.

"Yes, very recently, at least in terms of physics. I and a few other physicists began theorizing that there is a third kind of physics called the Holographic Universe Theory.

"That theory states that the entire universe operates exactly like a laser-generated Hologram. In making a Hologram, lasers are fired at a three-dimensional object and then directed onto a plate. This plate begins showing interference patterns just like if you throw several stones into a pond. Each stone creates a ring of waves on the surface of the pond. If they begin intersecting each other, interference patterns develop.

"In the case of Holograms, if another light is shined on the interference patterns, a three-dimensional Hologram appears. The image has no substance or location in the world, but it's there none-the-less. And that's what makes up our universe. It's called the Holographic Universe Theory.

"Everything in the Holographic universe is connected to a universal interference plate, so a gifted person like Jhona is able to trace the patterns back to the plate and manipulate so-called reality. If she is able to do that, it means she can manipulate our reality, change it any way she likes. If she can do that, she will possess terrific power—almost a godlike power.

"It's likely that partially exercising this power is what witches have actually done over the centuries. Because they didn't understand the elements of Holographic or quantum physics, they were limited in how much manipulation they could actually accomplish."

"What's the total, I mean how far could they take it?" asked Jeff.

"Well, in theory they could go so far as to totally change our universe."

"Change our universe?"

"Yes. According to the theory there are an infinite number of universes, all connected by the Holographic plate, and all accessible to a truly gifted person.

"Another cool thing is that if you break up the plate into smaller parts, the total image appears in each part. This implies that the total universe is contained in each particle including in every cell of our bodies and every sub-atomic particle. So, we're all totally connected with the infinite everything else.

"Some people call this the spiritual world, or as I prefer, paranormal physics."

"This is where we get into ghosts and things like that, and our tape?" asked Peter.

"Precisely, Peter. Ghosts and things like that. They're just as real, and just as weird as the Quantum world. They're part of the Holographic reality."

"But, how do we know Jhona has this kind of power?" asked Peter.

"We don't. Not yet anyway, but from what you have told me, I think she's a natural. The mysterious tape has just awakened the power within her. I'm pretty sure she will find ways to develop it further as time goes on."

"You mean as space time goes on," said Jeff.

"Now you're starting to get it," said Crullmar.

GO AROUND WITH MAD PEOPLE? OH, YOU CAN'T AVOID THAT HERE

"Can you take a little more explanation before we get to your tape?" Crullmar asked.

The boys nodded.

"Okay. So we theorize that there are distinctly different physics operating in our universe. There is some sort of a demarcation point where one set of physics rules fade and the other takes over. It's probably a non-dimensional line, and there is some evidence that it fluxes or varies slightly, so it can't really be pinpointed.

"The third factor, the Holographic physics is the basis of the other two and seamlessly connects them both. These forces may be used by skilled people like Jhona, but they may also be used by something we don't understand called dark energy. There is also dark matter. Do either of you know what these are?"

They both shook their heads.

"Good answer, absolutely accurate. No one knows what dark energy is or what dark matter is either, but the universe if full of it. In fact most of the universe is filled with dark matter. We think it is the power behind the third physics. The other two physics are powered by gravity and magnetic forces. We actually don't know much about those forces, either, but they could both be powered by dark energy.

"There are many examples of how this third physics has been operating within the other two. Take witchcraft for example. One of the proofs that someone was a witch back in the 1600s was if she was determined to be in two places at the same time. It was always a 'she' by the way.

"This was refuted a hundred years or so later as the world learned more about Newtonian physics. In those laws, dual states are not possible, but they are in Quantum states.

"Those of us who favor this three-physics theory feel that there is intelligence behind the dark energy. We think it's analogous to the force of life in our universe. In other words, it thinks, but very differently than we do. Some theologians who are interested in this theory think that the dark energy is an evil force while the Quantum/Newtonian forces are 'good.'"

"God versus the Devil? Good versus evil?" Peter asked.

"I'm afraid so," said the doctor. "Although many people, including myself, think of these two forces as different sides of the same coin. Actually, it's a coin with three sides. Try wrapping your mind around that concept."

"So those ghost voices are some sort of a manifestation of this dark energy," asked Peter.

"That's the theory."

"Not ghosts, then."

"Not very likely."

"Why do you say that, doctor?" Jeff asked.

"Well, when you examine all of the EVPs that have been recorded, you notice that none of the *ghosts* are at all articulate. More often than not they don't even address the questions put to them, and they can only manage three or four words, words that don't really make any sense.

"That doesn't mean that the dark energy is incapable of what we would call thinking. It is, and it can communicate in its own way. I believe that it manipulates the demarcation line to encompass people. That's how people become possessed. It's exactly the same way evolution on our scale occurs. The intelligence part of these two forces causes change in living things, such as plants, for example.

"Like how rosebushes grew thorns for protection against animals or how bees learned to gather pollen to pollinate plants and make food for themselves at the same time. We label these forces as being either for good or for evil. The thing to remember is that both forces are connected and part of our universe. They're all manifestations of the Holographic universe. They are just different aspects of reality.

"Okay, I think we are ready to listen to that tape of yours."

With everything set up, doctor Crullmar threaded the tape through the recorder heads and pressed play. At first the only sound was tape hiss. Crullmar pointed his pen at the laptop screen. Even the hiss was being displayed as a series of vertical lines similar to a Richter scale used to record seismic activity. They were pretty even in size with just a very small variation.

After a brief moment the audio portion of the tape began playing. It was the same interview the boys had heard in the library and both Dorothy's and Ruby's voices began scrolling across the screen.

BE AFRAID. BE VERY AFRAID

The tape rolled through the interview cleanly with no extraneous noises or voices. After listening to all of it, Crullmar turned the tape over and hit 'play' again. There were no voices on the second side, but the laptop display continued scrolling low-level sounds similar to those on the first side.

He placed the tape back in its box and cleared a space on his crowded desk. He then placed the tape box in the center of the cleared space.

"Okay, now men I want to show you something."

Crullmar slowly moved the box to one end of the cleared space.

"Notice how nothing happened when I slowly move the box from one side of this cleared space to the other. Now watch what happens when I move it rapidly from one side to the other."

He gave the box a vigorous shove. The box disappeared from view for an instant and then suddenly re-appeared on Crullmar's chair.

Peter and Jeff just stared at the box wide-eyed.

"Remember what I said? If you can see a Quantum object, you can't predict its path. If you can predict its path, you can't see it. So when we move a Quantum object, its path becomes unknown to us. What happened is that this tape has become 'captured' as it were by the dark Quantum force—even though by Quantum standards it is a very large piece of matter. It has been enveloped by the dark force."

Peter spoke up, "Can that happen to people, too?" His voice cracked just a little.

"We don't have any direct evidence of that, but there are stories. Remember what I told you about the witches being seen in two places at the same time? That's definitely dark force envelopment. It's possible that those witches had learned how to manipulate the dark forces.

130

That kind of manipulation was probably what they were doing when they cast 'spells.'"

"Could that be what was happening to Jhona when she claimed she was levitating?" asked Peter.

"Definitely. I think something is trying to capture her just as they did with the Salem witches. She could be in great danger, but before we can take steps to rescue her, we need to learn a bit more about this particular manifestation.

"Let's start by taking a look at these voice prints."

LOOK. LOOK INTO MY EYES

Crullmar carefully and slowly moved the tape from his chair and placed it in an empty 'out' basket on his desk. He then pulled his chair around so it was next to the boys and sat down.

"Let's see what we have here now," he said. "We'll start with the noise prints from side one." He opened the file. "Notice the noise prints running along the bottom of this file. That's the ambient noise picked up by Dorothy's recorder. It's composed of room noise, the sound of the recorder's motor, and any other stray sounds. That's where we are most likely to find our dark force artifacts."

Using his mouse, Crullmar magnified the small lines at the bottom of the screen and then moved them to a separate file. With these sounds isolated from the voices, Crullmar began running the file through his sound system. At first only a rumbling sound combined with a higher frequency hissing sound could be heard. Suddenly there was a definite spike in the noise.

Crullmar halted the playback and ran his mouse over that spike—back and forth. It sounded like a squeal. Next he drew a box around the spike sound and dropped it into another file. He then extended the lines horizontally until they filled the width of the new file. When that was completed, he let the file play through the audio system.

There was a voice. It was hard to understand, and it seemed to be composed of the hissing sound, like an articulation of the hissing. Crullmar stopped the playback.

"What's happening here is that the dark force has manifested itself into an actual entity of some sort. Having no vocal chords and being unable to speak, it uses the ambient tape hissing sound as its voice. I'm going to amplify it a bit more to see if we can understand what it is saying."

Crullmar adjusted the gain switch and let the voice roll again. The voice sounded like several different people speaking, each one saying a different syllable.

"Busted. You are busted Crulllllllmaaarrrr. Busted. You piece of shiiiiiiiiittttttt."

BROKEN THROUGH TO THE OTHER SIDE

"Well, it looks like we have a very grouchy entity today. Notice how it seems to be aware of what we are doing, and who we are. However, it doesn't quite have the strength to fully articulate in the way you or I can. Speech is very hard. Even for people. It's one of the first things to go when people are struck with serious or fatal diseases.

"Let's see how it goes on the second side of the tape."

Crullmar opened the 'side two' file and went through the same process with it that he had done with the first side. Soon he had isolated and amplified the vocals on that side. He let it play.

"Doktor Crrruuulll. What (unintelligible) doingggg dooonngg? Wehalf. Weeeehalffff JoJo. Jooogno. Jooogena. Wehalf herrrr."

"Okay," said Crullmar. "That's a threat. It is trying to work something through Jhona. She'll be safe as long as she stays in the hospital. Before we take any action on her behalf, I need to look at one other thing.

"I think because this is a tape made by Ruby the whole incident probably goes all the way back to Dallas, possibly all the way back to the Kennedy assassination. I think the entity Ruby mentioned was working the whole thing. It may have the ability to jump from person to person, but got bottled up somehow by Dorothy. Maybe, just maybe Dorothy killed herself as the only way to stop it, but it was able to jump back into the tape.

"The good thing is that there are a lot of good video records of that event and the subsequent killing of Oswald which may allow us to trace what's going on. Let's download a couple of things from the Internet."

Crullmar went to work at his laptop for a while. "Why don't you two go down to the cafeteria and grab us some coffee. This will take a while."

It was a great relief for the two boys to get out in the sunlight.

"What do you think about all that, Jeff?"

"Hey, Dude, I completely trust Crullmar. I've never met anyone who understands physics the way he does. And that audiotape. Dude, that's crazy stuff, and I mean *really crazy* stuff."

"Yes, and I'm getting concerned about this threat to Jhona, that whole concept of turning her into a witch. It's either totally bogus or totally terrifying. I can't decide which."

"You can't decide which? Which is the witch?"

"Not funny, Dude. Not in the slightest bit funny."

"Well, do you really think Jhona is possessed, or whatever Doctor Crullmar calls it?"

"I don't know, Dude. It's just that Jhona is not one to make things up like that levitation bit. I should never have doubted that. All I know is that I want to get through this stuff that the Doctor wants us to see so I can get back to her."

By the time the boys returned to the Doctor's office, he was all set up.

"OK, boys. Now I want you to watch these videos very carefully with me. First is the legendary Zapruder film of Kennedy's death. It's just over twenty-six seconds long, but it is the best record of the assassination." The video started rolling.

"Now, this is a short film, but notice right before Kennedy gets hit as his car moves in front of the grassy area, you will see lots of black flakes floating on the grass background. They look for all the world like bad spots in the film itself. However, I firmly believe that if the original film was closely examined, we would find those black flakes are photographed by the film and are not a part of it."

"What do you think they are, then?" Jeff asked.

"I believe they are Quanta particles that were attracted to the pending tragedy. Just like negative and positive charges being attracted to each other, only the attraction is between dark energy and light energy.

"My theory is those artifacts are like little sharks swarming around a bleeding man. Furthermore, I think this film represents the first time enlarged Quanta, powered by dark energy, have been photographed. I'd give just about anything to get hold of that original film, but it's locked up in the archives.

"Now take a look at the video of Ruby shooting Oswald. Notice how Ruby seems to be totally invisible to everyone. I'll stop the video right here where Ruby has emerged and is in the act of pulling the trigger. See how it looks like no one can see him? He's totally invisible to Oswald's guards even though he must have been closing in fast, and at least one of them should have been attracted to the movement. Even Oswald doesn't seem to see Ruby. If Ruby were infused with a Quantum state, he would have been invisible to all of them as he moved, which this frame proves, seems to indicate. Just like a Quantum particle is not visible when moving.

"In fact the whole time Ruby was wandering around the police garage, only one person seemed to have noticed him, and that person didn't think to question him. All he could do was to give Ruby a limp hello."

"So, you think Ruby was possessed by Quantum dark forces?" asked Peter.

"Yes. Look at this next frame. It shows the guards' faces as the gun goes off. They're surprised at the shot, sure, but they also have the look of, "where did *you* come from?" Was he invisible as he moved around through the crowd?

"Now notice all the space surrounding Oswald and Ruby as he materializes with his gun. Why were they all looking at everything but the approaching Ruby? He's isolated; he is even holding his gun out at arm's length."

"So if Ruby was invisible, why does he appear in the video?"

"Because Ruby was actually there. The film picks it up even though the people don't. It's a manifestation of the Quantum observer principal. Ruby was both there and not there. He both shot Oswald and didn't shoot him. The observation of him shooting set the reality to that, but no one could tell what the outcome was to be by observing Ruby before the shooting."

"How could Ruby have shot Oswald and not shot him?"

"That's just what we observe about Quantum states. We don't know why they happen, although there are plenty of theories out there. One of them states that there are many parallel universes. If, for example, you take a particular action, like walking out that door, in this universe you actually do walk through it, but there is a parallel universe where you don't, and both are equally real.

"Anyway, the Quanta photographed by the film is just a theory of mine. I can't prove it unless I could get possession of the actual film, and no one is going to ever let me do that."

ROUND MIDNIGHT

Peter's cell phone rang. He took the call and then looked up at them. "It's Jhona. She's being discharged in an hour. Jeff, we've got to go over and pick her up.

"Where is she?" asked Doctor Crullmar.

Peter answered, "She's over at St Francis Memorial, Bush and Hyde."

"That's clear across town. Tell you what. I'll give you a ride over. I'd like to talk with her if you don't mind."

"I don't mind," said Peter. "The key will be if *she* minds or not."

"Okay. I have a very good bedside manner."

Crullmar had just finished saying that when a startled look came over his face.

"Is Jhona about five-four with shoulder-length brown hair, and bangs?"

"That's right, doctor. Why do you ask?" Peter said.

"Because I just saw her, or at least I caught a glimpse of her. Just out of the corner of my eye, in the hallway there. It was an indistinct look, and she seemed to just quickly fade out, like a bad picture on an old television."

"She was there?" Peter was beginning to shake.

"Well, part of her was there," said the doctor. Remember what I said about witches being in two places at the same time? I think she has definitely been infected with dark energy, and some of this Quantum phenomenon is beginning to happen to her. I'm guessing she's surprised by it and doesn't know how to control it, but I'll bet she's beginning to like the feeling."

"We definitely need to get to the hospital, and fast," said Peter.

PICKUP STICKS

Jhona was becoming confused by a raft of new, very unusual sensations. If she lay back and let all of the tension in her muscles slide out of her body, a meditation technique she learned in her yoga class, she got a feeling like she was being slowly immersed in warm water. She could definitely feel the "wet line" move sensuously up her body until she was submerged.

She could breathe, and she didn't feel any sort of panic. In fact, she felt very warm and relaxed, like she was at total peace with the world. She could breathe easier, too. The pain from her lungs was gone. In fact, she could see a cloud of dark smoke emanating from her mouth as she breathed out. It kind of hovered above her like a flat, kind of 'T' shaped cloud. The bottom part of the 'T' was connected to her mouth, and she could feel it all the way into her lungs.

If she breathed in, the cloud would move back inside her, and if she breathed out, the cloud would form again.

She took a very deep breath and managed to get the entire cloud back inside her. She then blew out as hard as she could and the cloud came all the way out. Only now, as the cloud spread out, she felt as though she was in it, looking down at herself.

She panicked for a moment thinking she had died and was experiencing one of those out-of-body things that she had heard about.

She was out of her body for sure, but not dead. In fact she could move "her" arms and legs, turn her head…everything she had always been able to do. The only thing was, she was able to see her cloud self from her body at the same time she could see her corporeal self floating above. Corporeal self. Was that the correct word?

Her thoughts turned to Peter. Where was he?

As soon as that thought entered her mind, she felt it being transferred to her cloud self, and then, in an instant, she was standing in a wood-paneled hallway looking into a small, cluttered office. Inside were Peter and Jeff with their backs to her. They were talking to a black man with fuzzy white, no silver hair. The black man looked up and was startled, as he looked straight into Jhona's eyes.

Jhona was calm. She felt very, very powerful. She knew she could kill this black man if she wanted to. The thought frightened her, but it was also stimulating, erotically stimulating. She felt a need growing between her legs, a painful, urgent need, a need for release, a blood lust. Then, an orgasm coursed through both of her bodies.

The black man's expression changed to a kind of panic as though he could tell what was going on with her. In an instant, she was back in her hospital room. The smoke was receding into her mouth, back into the depth of her lungs. She fell deeply asleep.

THE ANGEL TOLD THE SHEPARDS NOT TO BE AFRAID

Jhona's doctor was very pleased at how quickly this young lady had recovered from her smoke inhalation. It was probably a testament to a healthy lifestyle that absolutely no bad effects were present after a couple of days in the oxygen tent. By the time the doctor had finished his report, her discharge was fully processed and she was sitting downstairs waiting in a wheelchair for her boyfriend to come pick her up. She was bored again.

For her part, Jhona felt it was ridiculous to make her wait in the lobby sitting in a wheelchair when she was perfectly okay. At least Peter should be coming in a few minutes.

Actually, she was in a very cross mood. Her head hurt, probably from reassuring her mother on the phone that she was okay and there was no need for her to fly out.

Every now and then, Jhona would think back to her experience in the hospital bed. Was it real? It seemed real. She could remember every moment of it with a kind of crystal clarity that she had never before experienced, especially the orgasm. That was the most amazing…suddenly Peter's goofy face was blocking her field of vision.

"Hey, babe. The doctor says you're OK. Ready to go home. How do you feel?"

"Oh, I feel great, just hunky-dory great. Never better in my life. How do you feel?"

"Um, I feel okay."

"You feel okay? Good. Then we both feel okay. How does our little friend there, Jeff, feel? Does Jeff feel okay, too?"

"Uh, yeah, Jeff feels fine. He, uh, actually didn't breathe in any smoke, so…"

"So, Jeff feels fine. That's great. Jeff feels fine because Jeff didn't crawl into the burning building to drag me to safety like you did. Right?"

"Well, that's…"

"Please. Give it up, Peter. Where are we going?"

"Well, our apartment will take a few days for the painters to finish, and we'll have to go through all our books and clothes and stuff to…"

"Could you just answer my question? Should I repeat it for you? *Where* are we going? Now. Right now. Where are we going *now*?"

"Okay. Now. Where are we going now? Fair enough. Okay. Right now we are going to the Hyatt in the Embarcadero. I've booked a nice room there for the next four nights. Does that sound alright…"

"Peachy. It just sounds peachy. So, how much is that going to cost?"

"Well, that's the good news. I've got an agreement with the owner, that is the owner of our apartment that he'll pay half…"

"Half? That's the best you could do? Half?"

"Well, Jhona. You left the teakettle on the stove. The only reason he's willing to pay half is because there were some code issues with the wiring, and…"

"Whatever. Whatever. I'm sure you've done the best you could. By the way, who is that guy over there? He keeps staring at me." Jhona pointed to Doctor Crullmar who was leaning on a trashcan listening to the conversation. She, of course, recognized him from her vision, but still didn't know exactly who *or what* he was.

Just as Peter was about to introduce the doctor, he walked over and held out his hand. Jhona made no move to take it. Instead she just stared coldly at him.

"Hello, Jhona. Nice to meet you," he said. His voice was somehow soothing, rich and deep." Jhona didn't react.

"My name is Doctor Crullmar. I'm a physicist, and I think I understand what you've been going through lately."

"You're a *physicist*, and you think you understand what *I've* been going through. *Lately*? What I've been going through? *Lately*?"

"Yes. If you like, I can discuss my theory with you on the ride to the hotel."

"Oh, goodie! Just what I hoped for. I'm just out of the hospital, and I get to have a physics lecture in a hot, greasy cab on the way to a hotel room where I'll be forced to stay until my boyfriend here, the absolute love of my life, decides which of our precious objects are too smoke damaged and have to be thrown away."

Meanwhile a cab pulled up to the curb, and nothing more was said until they were all seated inside. Jhona in the rear sandwiched between the doctor and Peter; Jeff in the front seat.

The weird foreign guy in the driver's seat jerked down the little flag, and with an indifferent look at the rushing oncoming traffic, he roared out into the stream.

IT'S TIME TO TALK OF MANY THINGS

It was a quiet ride to the hotel. Everyone was captured by their own thoughts, and it was obvious that Jhona, wedged in the middle of the back seat, was uncomfortable and didn't want to talk. She kept feeling like things were crawling on her legs, bugs, probably from the cab's filthy floor.

Just about when she thought she couldn't suppress a scream any longer, the cab lurched into the hotel driveway. They got out with collective sighs of relief, and the four of them stood in an uncomfortable group with Jhona suspiciously eyeing Doctor Crullmar as Peter paid the fare.

Crullmar broke the ice, "Peter, you're all checked in here, aren't you?" Peter nodded. "Then I suggest we go have some lunch in the restaurant here and talk about what is happening to Jhona."

"What are you? Some kind of therapist nut job?" Jhona said.

"I'll give you a whole rundown inside. Okay, Jhona?"

"Sure. Whatever."

Once they were seated and had ordered lunch, Doctor Crullmar explained his theory to Jhona. As a psyche major at UCSF, Jhona was more receptive to Crullmar's theories than either Jeff or Peter expected.

Just as Crullmar finished speaking, their lunch arrived. Jhona ate about half of her salmon, took a healthy swig of her Diet Coke and looked Crullmar straight in the eye. "That's exactly what's been happening to me."

Without saying another word, she looked down and consumed the rest of her fish with Jeff and Peter staring at her.

"Jhona. Wha…" Peter stammered. "More things have been happening to you?"

"Yeah, Peter. More things have been happening to me. Did I mention that I can now astral project myself anywhere I want?"

"No, you…didn't…"

"Well, I've been practicing and I've gotten very good at it. All I have to do is breathe deeply and think about some place I'd like to be, and then, *BAM.* There I am. Jeff, will you pass the salt, please?"

Jeff, startled at being addressed by Jhona knocked over the shaker. When he looked over at Jhona, she was using it to salt her green beans. The knocked-over shaker was no longer lying on the little pile of salt. If fact, the little pile of salt was gone. As thought it had never existed.

"See?" said Jhona. "I'm getting pretty good at doing a lot of cool things. I guess I'm a witch now." She threw a glaring look at Peter. "Can you deal with that, *Dude*?"

Peter tried talking, but could only generate a little squeaking sound. Jhona looked at him for a second and said, "Close your mouth, Peter. You look like an idiot."

WHICH WITCH IS WHICH

Doctor Crullmar broke the confused silence. "Jhona." Jhona looked up at him with an amused expression on her face. He really was tall. Even sitting down he seemed to tower over everyone. And that silver Afro, it was like a magnificent silver crown, and his skin was a coppery black. It was shiny and reminded her of a copper plate her grandparents had brought back from a trip to Greece years ago. It had been hand-worked to shine with a magnificent patina. Her grandfather described it as being priceless. "Look at it, Jhona, and see the work that went into it. See the perfection of the result. If you look at it long and hard enough, you'll be able to see the future."

"You'll be able to see the future, Jhona." She was both thinking and hearing the words. Her eyes were locked on the doctor's. She was aware of the two boys sitting at the table, but they seemed suspended and covered by a cloudy mist. They were irrelevant.

Her thinking and the doctor's voice resonated together. One was the same as the other. Only the doctor's eyes existed for her. The gaze was opening up something all around her, something vast and dark and certain, yet uncertain. Soon she saw and felt the infinity beyond her, the vastness of the universe with its exploding stars—and something more—its black holes.

She was in a small boat. A canoe. And she was in a black stream. It was flowing gently towards something, something vast. She was able to resist the gentle stream that was pulling her towards…it was a black hole. She was sure of that, a crushing, infinite black hole.

The Doctor's voice was there in the canoe with her. "Jhona. Keep paddling. Don't allow yourself to be taken by the current to the point of no return. If you do, you will be sucked into the blackness. All your atoms will be compressed so that there will be no space in them. You will become solid matter and will never be able to escape."

Jhona kept up her gentle paddling. She turned the canoe around so she could look on the black hole and paddled backwards. It was beautiful in its total blackness. She could see the swirling madness of matter, energy, and time itself being sucked into it. She was mesmerized, and the thought occurred to her that with all that destruction, she should be able to hear something. But there was only silence.

As she gazed at the hole she began to realize that it wasn't a hole at all, but the tape reel; the Ruby interview. It was so large; the size of a million galaxies. She could barely see the curve of the reel. But it was the tape. That was for sure.

She began hearing the voices of the interview. They were loud and seemed to fill a vast amount of space, but in the background was the doctor's voice. So faint, but so insistent. What was he saying? She focused on it…tried to block out the *big* voice.

"Come back now, Jhona. It's time to come back. Paddle to my voice. You must do it, Jhona. Come back to me."

She turned the canoe around and began to frantically paddle back. She was making slow progress, but as she got further away from the point of no return, the Doctor's voice got louder, and her progress back up the stream became faster and easier.

****

"Now open your eyes, Jhona. Open them and look at me."

She opened her eyes. Her head was down on the table, and she had been drooling. She lifted her head up. The doctor was staring at her with those eyes, those intense eyes.

"Very good, Jhona. You must always listen to what I say."

Jhona couldn't speak. She just looked into those eyes and nodded her head.

"Remember. Every black hole has an *event horizon*. That's the point at which nothing can escape the crushing pull of its gravity. Not light, not thought. Nothing. But before the event horizon is the point of no return. Do you know what that is, Jhona?"

Jhona shook her head. The Doctor was beautiful, so beautiful, and his voice was like liquid gold. She enfolded every word, caressed every word like a new baby. With love and caring. Gentle caring.

"Jhona. Listen to what I'm saying. That stream you were in—vast amounts of particles being sucked into the hole. It's mostly dark matter. You were in that stream, the part of you that had separated from your body. You were approaching the point of no return.

"Think of it like rowing on a river just before a huge waterfall. There is a point before the actual falls where no matter how hard you paddle, you will not be able to paddle fast enough to avoid going over the falls. For you the falls were really the event horizon. Got it?"

Again Jhona nodded absently. Her entire body hurt. Especially her head, but she understood. At least that part she understood. What exactly had happened to her she didn't understand. What was going on? Something scary, but wonderful.

"You'll travel there again, Jhona, but you'll need to remember this truth. It's the most important truth of all. And that is that you won't know when you've passed the point of no return. Everything in the stream will seem fine. You'll be drifting along peacefully. The only sign that you are approaching that dangerous point is that you will be moving a little faster, every second, a little faster. Just listen for my voice. I'll warn you. You must always listen for my voice. Do you understand, Jhona?"

Jhona nodded absently. Doctor Crullmar dipped a napkin into a glass of water and wiped some of the mascara that was running down her face. She was crying, or at least tears were running down her face.

There was no sobbing. No unhappiness. In fact she felt good, very good, better than she had ever felt before; so powerful, so very, very powerful. She knew she could do things now that she had been to the black hole, all kinds of things. Things she had never imagined that she or anyone else could do.

"Jhona," the doctor snapped his fingers.

"Jhona, stop thinking about that. Look at me. Stop thinking about your power. I need you back in the world now. Can you come back? All the way back?"

"Yea...yesss," she said. He was so beautiful with that silver Afro. It even crackled as little sparks ran through it. His face looked like it had been chiseled out of solid granite. As she looked, the granite began cracking and crumbling until there was only his kind, human face.

PETER, PETER, PUMPKIN EATER

Jhona was all the way back to reality now. Peter and Jeff were talking to Doctor Crullmar as though nothing had happened. She had a million questions, but she sat there in silence. They must have ordered food because the waiter drifted over and put plates of food in front of everyone. Hers consisted of a perfect Mediterranean chicken wrap with alfalfa sprouts, slices of tomatoes, and avocado pieces. She began eating as she listened to what Crullmar was saying.

"…people come along once in a while who are able to tap into the strong, dark forces that run like an underground river beneath our reality. If these people showed the powers they accumulated from the dark forces, they were branded as witches and then suffered all manner of torture and painful deaths.

"Over the years, witches have learned how to mask these powers by claiming that Wicca, what they call magic these days, is a simple spiritual women's movement dedicated to getting in touch with the positive, healing powers that course through the earth. And that's true, for the most part, but sometimes they tap into the dark force, which is generated by strong currents of dark energy.

"This is not imagination. Scientists know dark energy and dark matter exist. Not only that, but most of the universe is made up of those two dark elements.

"This particular strand of the dark current…the one we are dealing with today…it's been around for a long time. It kind of searches, if that's the right word, it searches for receptive people.

"So, fifty years ago it found a perfect receptor, Lee Harvey Oswald. This force infused him with a desire to make a 'name' for himself through the old tried and true method of assassination. The dark force worked hard to create the opportunity—the presidential route, Oswald's place of employment, his marksmanship skills, and a ton of other elements that came together with three shots from that book depository.

"It was a mammoth effort for sure, but well within the capabilities of the dark energy because it works by subtly influencing human thought and actions.

"Remember when we viewed the Zapruder film and saw all those dark flecks moving along with the car? That was a rare visible manifestation of dark energy at work.

"Then along came Ruby. His hatred for Oswald opened the door for dark elements. According to Ruby's own testimony, he was possessed and driven by what he called demons."

"Wait, Dude," said Jeff. "Ruby didn't say he was driven, just possessed. They kept talking to him inside his head. He said he thought it was himself talking even though he knew he had been possessed."

"Yeah," Peter almost said the word, 'dude' but somehow it seemed too juvenile considering the circumstances. "And what about the threat to Dorothy at the end of the tape. She killed herself, remember?"

"Killed herself, or was killed," said Jeff. "No one knows which."

"That's the crux of the matter," said Crullmar. "Had Dorothy become a witch? Like it or not, folks, that's what has happened to Jhona, and we have to help her through it."

"I still don't understand," said Jhona. "Why was I in a particle stream heading for a black hole? Why did the black hole look like the tape reel? What was I doing there?"

"Okay, Jhona, I'll do my best to explain it. Our theories and understanding of black holes are changing all the time. There are things we know about them and things we just theorize about them.

"Among the things we know about them is that they do exist. Most physicists agree there is a massive black hole at the center of each galaxy. These monsters work like giant vacuum cleaners continuously sucking in matter from surrounding stars and growing larger all the time.

"One of the theories is that in addition to these monster black holes, there are billions and billions of micro black holes, many of which are too small to be seen by the naked eye. Their small size makes it easier for them to be manipulated by the dark energy forces that surround us. Jhona, you were able to see one of these up close. In fact, I believe it is the same one being used to control you, and the same one used to control Oswald, Ruby and Dorothy.

"The fact that you were guided to the tape-reel black hole is all the proof I need that you are being targeted by the dark energy forces. If they manage to project you onto the particle stream again, and then lull you enough so you slip beyond the point of no return, you will be captured by them. There will be no escape."

"What can we do?" There was just a touch of panic in Jhona's eyes.

"We'll have to develop your power. You've felt some of it already. If you can learn to manipulate the transition zone as effectively as the dark energy forces can, you'll be able to concentrate your own energy to push the zone back below the Newtonian/relativity border. That will completely diffuse the dark energy, but there will still be a threat."

"What threat?" Jhona asked.

"The threat of addiction. Addiction to your power. It sounds like a cliché, but it's true. Each time you use your power it corrupts your, uh, let's just call it your core. The very part of your existence that keeps you firmly rooted onto this side of reality."

"So...what? I might just drift off?"

"If your core determination to live in the reality zone is diffused enough, you would just let yourself drift through the point of no return and into the event horizon. The black hole provides a different kind of existence. No one knows what happens there, but it takes a lot of willpower to not want to just drift into it and find out. It's probably a lot like heroin or crack. You want that rush, but the more you use, the more you need to use."

"When can we start the training?" Jhona asked.

"Let's pay the bill here, and let you and Peter get settled in your room. I'm going to need some help, and I know just the right person."

HEY, BABY WON'T YOU TAKE A CHANCE?

Jhona and Peter said goodbye to Jeff and the doctor. In the elevator on the way up to their room, Jhona looked at their reflection in the polished surfaces of the copper-lined panels, just the two of them. She leaned her head against Peter's chest and closed her eyes. Peter felt good, a strong presence. There was a lot of strength in his warm embrace, and it was a sincere strength. She wondered about her own strength. Where was it?

The elevator continued its slow rise, bumping gently against the side of the shaft, the muffled whirring sound of the cable a comforting background noise. She looked up again at the reflections. She was looking at that infinity thing that parallel mirrors present, an endless number of Peters and Jhonas.

She looked as far as she could at the endless line. She noticed something way back in the farthest image. A shifting. The smallest Jhona and Peter had stepped out of line and were staring right at Jhona. Then the next image did the same thing. Then all of the images were moving out of line and beginning to circle like a vortex. Swirling around them in the polished surface—faster and faster, another goddamn hallucination. She was getting sick of them. She wanted to be left alone.

She raised her hands and closed her eyes. She made a pushing motion with her hands and felt a kind of recoil. As though she had fired off a pair of powerful handguns. The recoil rocked her, and she opened her eyes. There was a smell like something was burning.

The images were gone. Peter was sitting on the floor with a scared look on his face.

"Jhona. What the fuck?"

Jhona took a deep breath and said, "Sorry, Peter. I just…I don't know…it was… Are you okay?"

"I'm okay. Are you okay? That's the question. What the hell did you do?"

"I just had to make them go away."

"Make who go away?"

"Them. The reflections. They were circling. Just like doctor Crullmar said. They were trying to draw me in...*us* in."

"Well, are they gone now, Jhona?" Peter was beginning to think this chick was spookier than he ever imagined.

"They're gone now, Peter."

"Well that's good because this is our floor." Peter shook his head and rolled his eyes.

As they stepped out onto the carpeted hallway, Jhona looked back over her shoulder at the elevator. There was no elevator, just a dark shaft that fell away hundreds of feet.

"Figures," Jhona said to herself.

"Figures? What figures, Jhona?"

"Nothing," Jhona replied as Peter put the card into the slot. "Nothing at all, Peter. Nothing at all."

THE WILD SURF

Much to Jhona's surprise, she and Peter had a nice, uneventful evening. The next morning they met Doctor Crullmar for breakfast down in the hotel coffee shop. It was a beautiful day with lots of sun and many cheerful birds. They decided to take breakfast on the outside tables.

After the waiter cheerfully took their orders, and they had been left with a carafe of hot, strong coffee, Crullmar asked if everything was OK. Jhona decided not to mention anything about the elevator incident. Peter was a bit surprised at that, but he decided it was Jhona's "thing," and decided not to say anything either.

"Alright," Doctor Crullmar said. "I've made an appointment with the foremost expert on Quantum lines of departure. She's a psychologist with an office right next door on the 36th floor of Embarcadero One. She can give us two full hours today, which is very good luck."

"Can Jeff join us?" asked Peter. "You know, since he has been involved from the beginning."

"That's a great idea, Peter. In fact I was going to mention that myself. Go ahead and give him a call."

Nine o'clock found them in a small waiting room decorated with a tasteful collection of African artifacts – mostly wooden carvings and colorful textiles. Crullmar had disappeared into the office door to provide the psychologist with a rundown on what they were hoping to accomplish that morning. After about ten minutes had passed, Jeff entered the room looking around nervously.

"Morning, Dudes," he said.

"Good morning, Jeff," said Peter. Jhona smiled and nodded at him, but she was in no mood for chitchat, so she said nothing.

After another ten minutes had passed, Crullmar motioned for them all to enter the Doctor's office. They were all shocked at the scene inside.

156

The room was dark, and it took a few moments for their eyes to adjust. Four comfortable looking leather chairs faced each other in a circle. There were full-sized carved figures of abstract, African female forms, each in starkly sexual poses. Some were obviously pregnant while others were in squatting positions giving birth.

But the most startling scene was standing next to Doctor Crullmar in front of a wooden desk. Next to him was a beautiful female who was obviously his twin sister.

She was just an inch or two shorter than him, but her complexion matched his exactly. The facial structure was virtually the same except that hers was a finer, feminine version. However, the most startling thing about them was her hair. It was exactly the same—a full, gorgeous Afro just as bright silver as his. It was as though they were looking at twin, full moons.

IT'S A SISTER THING

After a brief and somewhat uncomfortable silence, Doctor Crullmar spoke up. "I'd like you all to meet my sister, Annabelle Silver. Annabelle, this is Jhona, Peter—Jhona's boyfriend, and Jeff, friend to both. Annabelle is both a psychiatrist and a fully certified witch. She's a master of the manipulation of the zones. She'll be your guide, Jhona while I'll be your protector."

Annabelle advanced to Jeff. She grabbed both of his shoulders and looked straight into his eyes for a full ten seconds. She then smiled and moved to Peter and did the same. Then she came to Jhona. Instead of taking her shoulders, she gently took both of her pale hands into hers. "You're shaking, Jhona. There's nothing to be afraid of here."

Jhona broke eye contact with Annabelle and looked down at her hands. Annabelle's hands were long and thin, and much larger than Jhona's. In fact Jhona's hands were so small compared to Annabelle's that they almost seemed to have disappeared into the warm, folds of Annabelle's dark, black skin.

As she looked, her hands actually were melding into Annabelle's flesh. Jhona became aware of an old clock ticking away. She couldn't place where the clock was, and she couldn't tear her eyes away from the vision of her hands melting into Annabelle's.

The clock's ticking began slowing down until it seemed there was a tick only every minute or so. Jhona felt herself being sucked into Annabelle's body. The hands had absorbed her all the way up to her elbows, and she was still moving into Annabelle. Each tick of the clock took her an inch or two inside. Then came a flash of bright light. Jhona and Annabelle were holding hands like figures in a Chagall painting. Slightly distorted and they were floating, their arms melted into each other's. Jhona felt Annabelle lift her arms up to eye level, and Jhona's arms followed.

Now they were looking at each other, eye-to-eye, across the circle formed by their arms. Still floating, they began rotating in a circle with the axis at the center of the circle.

Jhona heard Annabelle say, "Look down, Jhona, into the circle. Look deep into the circle." The voice was beautiful, kind of like small bells ringing.

Jhona was afraid. She shook her head and heard a distorted sound come from her mouth. "Noooooooo. Please…"

"Look *down*, Jhona. Look deeply into the circle. Do it *now*." The last word sounding as though a very large bell had been struck. The bell sound was moving past her, and she could hear the Dolby effect of it changing tone as it moved away from her, like a bell on a train.

She looked.

DO YOU TRUST ME? YOU CAN, YOU KNOW

The scene in the office seemed just as weird to Peter and Jeff as it must have to Jhona. There was Annabelle and Jhona holding hands at eye level, making a kind of circle. The circle itself was extended into a cylinder that went all the way from their arms into the floor. It seemed solid, but neither of them could tell what it was made of.

Doctor Crullmar was standing directly behind his sister. In a moment he began raising his arms and placed them on his sister's shoulders. As soon as he did that, wicked looking little sparks began crackling from his sister's silver Afro into his. Each crack was about as loud as a small firecracker, and they reminded Peter of the Chinese New Year.

"Why do the Chinese blow off firecrackers at New Year's," he thought. *"Why, of course, to frighten away evil spirits."*

As soon as that thought had passed through his mind there was one loud crackle and both Jhona's and Annabelle's hands dropped to their sides. The cylinder was gone.

Doctor Crullmar spoke first, "Let's have a seat everyone." He walked over to the little mini-fridge that had been cleverly disguised as a thickly woven African basket and pulled out four bottled waters.

"Drink this down. It'll help get the copper taste out of your mouth. Jhona, are you feeling OK?"

"I don't know…" she replied. Her voice was shaking a bit. "I looked, and I saw…I saw…"

"Take it easy, Jhona," said Annabelle. "Drink the water down. That will help."

Jhona gulped down half of the water and then wiped her mouth on a tissue Annabelle handed her.

"Feel better?" Annabelle asked. Jhona nodded. "Tell us what you saw, Jhona. Take your time."

160

"The hole. It was a cylinder. I could see way down it. There was no end to it, but the walls had, like, pictures on them. We were on the walls as though a projector was playing movies of us. It was like that talking head at Disneyland…in the haunted house."

"You mean the Hologram, Jhona?" asked Doctor Crullmar.

"Hologram?" said Jhona. "Yes it was. Just like a Hologram. I could see the whole room and everything outside of it."

"What you've seen is the universe as a Holographic projection. That's a theory, but you've actually seen it, Jhona. That makes you a visionary.

"The Holographic projection of the universe was proposed by physicist, Juan Maldacena. He theorized that gravity is created by vibrating strings much smaller than neutrons or protons. They come in and out of existence in nine space dimensions and one time dimension somehow creating the universe as a Hologram.

"You couldn't see the strings, because they are much smaller than light photons, but your astral projection has a way of seeing things without the need for light to bounce off them. Essentially you have the ability to project yourself into one of the other nine dimensions. That's where you will see the strings. They all vibrate and probably look a lot like worms or like the black artifacts we saw on the Zapruder film.

"Since you can also see the Holographic structure of the universe itself, with a little practice, you should be able to identify the exact dark energy forces we're dealing with and block them with your powers.

"That's what witches do, Jhona," said Annabelle. "When they cast spells, they are influencing and re-directing the vibrating gravitational strings. That's what you've got to learn how to do."

161

"Learn how to do what exactly?" said Jhona. "I don't understand any of this. How am I supposed to learn how to, what again? Block vibrating strings that look like wiggling worms?"

"We will help you," said Annabelle. "We'll be your guides on this side of the zone, but you'll need to find a guide on the other side, the Quantum side. We will help you do that as well."

"Annabelle and I will organize a coven of witches we trust. They'll be able to provide security for your 'beings' on both sides of the zone. You'll be safe and will be able to search for your guide on the other side."

Jhona had never been less sure of anything in her life, but she nodded her head. "Go ahead. Organize the witches. I'm as ready as I will ever be, I guess."

"Hey. Wait a minute," said Peter. "Now we're getting involved with witches? When did that happen? Jhona, you don't have to do this."

Doctor Crullmar looked at Peter and said, "Jhona has no choice, Peter. You're already involved with witches. We all are. Bad witches. Witches who want to capture Jhona and drag her across the zone into the Quantum realm. If the dark energy can capture her astral self, it will make them stronger."

"Her astral self, Doctor?" said Jeff. "Don't you mean her soul?"

"Well said, Jeff. Precisely. Her very soul is at stake."

IF I HAD A HAMMER

Since it had been determined that Jhona was a target for the dark energy elements, Doctor Crullmar decided to keep the Ruby tape until the coven could be convened. Annabelle thought it would be safest if it were placed in an ancient African witch doctor's 'poke.' The voodoo 'poke' had been given to Annabelle in New Orleans back when she was a skinny, knobby-kneed novice.

The voodoo doctor had taken pity on the lanky young girl because he knew that someone like her would become a likely target for any number of miscreants. Many an evil, opportunistic sneer had faded with one look at the bag hung from her skinny shoulder.

Annabelle had never used the bag to conceal a possessed object like the tape. Especially not one that possibly contained a micro-black hole and was being used by strong dark energy forces to possess someone. On the other hand, Voodoo was a very strong force, and Annabelle had long believed that it was a very effective way to deal with forces from the Quantum side.

The bag was made to contain powerful magical objects used in voodoo rituals. The idea was that a voodoo witch doctor could place the objects into the bag and not have to worry about them until they were needed.

The most obvious and well known of these was the ubiquitous voodoo doll. A visitor to the Big Easy could purchase one in a variety of colors and sizes at any of the millions of souvenir shops in town. Annabelle had even seen life-sized dolls for sale.

A true voodoo doll was another thing entirely. It took weeks to construct one, and that wasn't counting the additional weeks it took to gather all the spices, chicken blood and host of other disgusting items that went into the making of the dolls and infusing them with magical powers.

The doll, like many other magical objects, couldn't just be made and then put on a shelf somewhere. They had to be controlled least the magic powers so carefully infused in them leak out and lessen. Or even worse, become absorbed by the voodoo doctor.

Yes, arguably the most powerful practitioners of voodoo were the female witches. Females always seemed to be the most adept at these arts, and Annabelle was legendary among witches for her power and control over the arts.

Annabelle's witch's bag was woven with a special reed fabric that had been planted during the full moon closest to the summer equinox in a year ending with an eight. Naked, and menstruating fourteen-year-old girls prepared the ground for planting by allowing their blood to fall onto the dirt as they bent over to place the seeds in the consecrated dirt. And that was just for the reeds.

Weaving the reeds into a bag required many other careful, time-consuming rituals. The most powerful aspect in constructing the bag involved making the mystic designs on both the inside and outside of the bag itself. It was rumored that a well-made bag required the sacrifice of more than one animal, and some rumors said that the blood of a newborn baby also needed to be shed onto the bag.

Whatever the truth was of the bag's construction, Annabelle had immense faith in its ability to keep spells, both white and dark, fully contained.

As she placed the tape onto her small voodoo alter she noticed that it felt very cold. That was a bad sign, so she quickly opened her bag and spit inside it while reciting a spell. Placing the open bag next to the tape, she swept it into the recesses of the bag and quickly closed it.

The temperature in her office noticeably dropped. She glanced at the thermometer on her desk. Fifty-five degrees. Down from seventy-two. She'd never seen that kind of a drop before. If the bag couldn't hold the spell inside, she was in for trouble. Big trouble.

I'VE GOT TO START WRITING STUFF DOWN

At that moment Doctor Crullmar was walking back to Annabelle's office after having used the restroom. As he approached the office door, he felt the hairs on his head begin to rise. They were becoming infused with static electricity just like when he and Annabelle went into a state.

He hurried into her office. Annabelle was laying on the floor in a fetal position. Her hand was inside the open bag and it was convulsing as though she were trying to grab something.

"The *tape*," thought Crullmar. "Annabelle. Let go of the tape. Let go of it."

Annabelle opened her mouth. A gush of crimson blood flowed out onto the floor. She began coughing and sat up, her hand out of the bag now.

Crullmar moved quickly to her side. Kicking the bag across the floor, he placed her head on his lap.

"You'll be OK, Sis. Go ahead and throw up if you have to. Look, I'll go get you a paper towel and a cup of tea. Can you talk?"

"Yes," she said, but the effort caused her to begin coughing. "After her coughing spell was over, she looked up at her brother and said, "Yes. Please. Get me some tea. I'm okay."

Crullmar was able to make fast work with the tea because the office break room had an instant hot water dispenser. The room was shared by all the offices on the floor, so he felt lucky that he didn't run into anyone else. He quickly returned with the tea and a wad of paper towels.

Annabelle was sitting in her desk chair when Crullmar entered the room. Her head was below her knees. "Joey," she said in between daubing her mouth and sipping the tea. "What were we thinking? We can't access this without a full coven. And we'll need heavy duty protection at that."

"Do we even know anyone who can watch our backs while we're in there?"

Annabelle coughed a few more times. "We'll have to go to New York. That contact we met at last year's gathering…what was her name? You know the one I'm thinking about."

"How could I forget? Samantha Idaho. We, uh, spent some quality time together."

"Really? I thought she was a lesbian."

"Well, she actually was, but…"

"I don't want to hear about that, but I think she's the only one serious enough about witchcraft to protect us. Do you still have her number?"

"Sure. In my office."

"You go call her, and tell the kids. Make reservations for all of us. Let your girlfriend back there know that this is an emergency situation with very powerful and unpredictable elements."

"Consider it done. I'll contact you tonight."

"What are we going to do with the tape?"

"As soon as you feel better, we'll both seal it in the bag. I think we can manage it if we don't touch the tape and we create a magic circle around it and the bag before we seal it up."

The bag-sealing ritual was conducted with no problems. Crullmar found himself thinking that the tape actually had a conscious mind behind it, and that mind was anxious to return to New York.

"You know, Annabelle, the tape really didn't start exhibiting Quantum powers until it came into contact with Jhona. According to the boys, it sat inside that box in the lawyer's office for fifty years, and no one even knew it was in there."

"Yes, as soon as Jhona came in contact with it the Quantum broadcasting began."

"Right, Sis. It's almost as though there is another group of, dare I say it…witches working against us. Someone must have sensed the power in that tape. Who, though? Who have they come in contact with since they received the package?"

"That's an easy one to answer, Joe. Remember their trip to the library? The assistant who kept hanging around…"

"Yes, and neither he nor the little room were there when they went back again."

"Well, okay. We'll just have to watch our back."

"That's going to get harder to do, Sis. That tape is gaining strength as it sucks in more power."

"Yes, the curse of a black hole drawing in dark energy. It just gets stronger. Do you think the bag can contain it for the entire trip back east?"

"There's no way to tell. It was dormant during its initial trip out here, but now…I just don't know."

"I hate flying. Look, I think we all need to split up. How about if I fly with Jhona, and you take the bag and Peter and Jeff?"

"No, that might yield some bad consequences. I think the tape is giving Jhona her strength, and she is getting very, very strong. She doesn't even realize yet just how strong she is. Now she just needs to learn how to use it. I think she's going to need as much strength as she can get."

"Yeah. Maybe. It still scares me, though."

"It's scary, but I think the tape is a talisman for her. A talisman so powerful that the other side has become aware of it and wants it very badly."

"The other side. God help us."

DIRTY DEEDS DONE AT A DISCOUNT

Jhona loved flying and began relaxing for the first time in days. Looking out the window at the beautiful land far below made her feel like she had borrowed the eye of God for a few hours.

The people below seemed so insignificant. You couldn't even see an actual person until you got down to a few hundred feet. Even the buildings seemed tiny and dwarfed compared to all the mountains and rivers.

Of course the effects of humans were always in evidence. Once a town spread out enough to become a major city, the buildings began looking more like an infectious disease than anything. And there were towns everywhere. Nestled up against mountain ranges, lakes, rivers, anywhere there was water it seemed.

She wondered what it must have looked like two hundred years ago when there were only a handful of big cities and no automobiles or airplanes. Of course no one back then had the view she was now enjoying, and that was only two hundred years ago. Not much time, really, when you think about it.

And now, here she was flying at, what, four hundred miles per hour, and at thirty-five thousand feet in the air clear across the continent. All because of a stupid audiotape filled with, what was it, dark energy. None of it made a lick of sense, that's for sure. And witchcraft? Jhona shot a quick glance at Annabelle. Annabelle, who did not at all appreciate flying, had her seat back as far as it would go and had placed a damp washcloth over her eyes; brave, witchy Annabelle.

Every now and then she would tremble slightly. She always said she was OK, just a little chill, but that didn't fool Jhona. She knew what was going on. It was that damn tape, and Annabelle was afraid of it.

Well, Jhona wasn't afraid of a little piece of shit tape. What the fuck, it didn't even reveal anything new about the Oswald assassination. It was the same old bullshit. She could still hear Ruby's voice in her mind. "I acted alone…was possessed by a demon." Such crap. She pitied the demon who tried crossing her in the morning before she'd had her first cup of tea. Just ask Peter what that's like.

She looked out the window again. Down below was a small town right next to a mountain range. She could see that it had recently snowed—a late spring snow. She could see the pattern of the fall, heavy over the slope up to the mountains, and thinning out to the west where it spanned a river and dissipated. She was getting sleepy…looking down at the snowfall…

Gradually she became aware that she wasn't in the airplane any longer. She was walking through thick woods. They were a mix of deciduous trees and thin, lodge-pole pines. The pines were still green, but the deciduous trees all had leaves that were a bright mix of fall colors, even though it was early spring. *"Curious,"* she thought to herself.

As she walked, colorful leaves fell from the trees flooding the path she was walking on with such intense color that she felt as though she were in an oil painting. Some of the leaves stuck to her shoulders and the bulky sweater she was wearing. When did she put on a sweater? She didn't even own a sweater like this one.

There was something beginning to cover the leaves. It crunched under her feet. Snow. She had walked into a thin layer of snow. Soon the snow completely covered the leaves. Her feet crunching the snow was the only sound. It was peaceful, so incredibly peaceful.

Then a very light snow began falling. The trees were all bare now. There were no more pines, only birches and aspens, their white trunks so thick. Jhona could only see three or four feet in any direction. The falling snow was incredibly beautiful, and peaceful.

As she moved farther into the forest, she noticed a thinning ahead. It was snowing harder now. Something was up ahead. She emerged onto the edge of a meadow. It was completely covered in snow, and more snow was falling now. There was no sound. She felt like she might have become completely deaf, but her feet still made a quiet crunching sound.

The meadow was circular…a huge, perfect circle. It was hundreds of yards to the edge, and every perimeter was blocked by the thickest trees she had ever seen. It was absolutely quiet and peaceful. But there was something in the center of the white circle, something round and black.

It was far away from Jhona, but it looked like the entrance to a cave, perhaps. It was pitch black. That was the right description. Pitch black. Not just black, but an absence of all color and texture.

"Fuck," Jhona thought. *"In all this peaceful beauty another goddamn black hole."*

I UNDERSTAND THE MAGIC THAT YOU DO

Jhona stood there at the edge of the beautiful meadow trying to figure out what to do. The peace of the meadow was pulling at her. She wanted more than anything else in her life to walk to the very center of that meadow. But what was that blackness? The meadow reminded her of a soul, perfect but for one black desire, the desire for witchcraft. Wasn't that what it was all about for her, now? Wasn't she a witch now? Isn't that what Doctor Crullmar and his freaky sister were saying?

A desire for witchcraft; what was that anyway? It was about power, that's for sure, the power over nature. Power to do your will. Whatever you wanted to do. Kill the President of the United States? No problem. You could do it without thinking about it twice, and then wonder, as Oswald must have done, what was all the fuss about?

Or Ruby. Kill the guy who killed the President. Easy. Fun. Powerful. No regrets. Change history forever.

So what was little Dorothy's problem? She seemed to be more of a victim than... a witch? Why wasn't she a witch? What happened to poor little Dorothy anyway? She certainly had enough self-confidence. Got the only private interview with that Ruby asshole. She was going to break open the entire JFK assassination case, or so she said. That took some power.

But then, dead. Suicide? Well that sure as batfuck wasn't going to happen to Jhona. No fucking way.

Jhona noticed that the whole time she was thinking about things she had been walking toward the black spot. She was only about three yards from it now, the white of the meadow all around her. The edges of which were so far away that she could just barely make out the trees that ringed it.

She took a few more steps toward the blackness, stopping an arm's length from the black spot. It looked like a tar pit, but it was beginning to move. Swirling. That's what it was doing. Swirling. But gathering itself and rising up. It was a figure, a human figure, but all black and shiny, a woman's figure.

The mouth was opening and closing as though it was trying to speak. Then Jhona noticed that the figure was Dorothy, and she was saying her name over and over, but with no sound.

A hand reached out to Jhona. It was black and shiny like tar. It took hold of Jhona's hand and raised it up, the hand intertwining with Jhona's fingers. Jhona could feel nothing. The hand was there, but it wasn't. Dorothy was beautiful.

Jhona became aware of the words. "I'm the black queen, but you, you are the white queen."

With that, Dorothy slid inside Jhona through her hand. When she was completely gone, Jhona looked at her hand. It was black, but it felt powerful. Jhona clasped her hands together, one black and the other white. She intertwined her fingers and faced her palms out.

She gave a little push, and a powerful shockwave emanated from her palms and went shooting across the meadow vaporizing the snow and knocking down all the trees on the other side.

****

The ground and sky undulated for a few seconds, and then Jhona felt a presence surrounding her. It was just outside of the periphery of the trees. She couldn't see anything, but she felt a strong *challenging* presence. A black shadow flew around the circle three times. Then it hovered over the downed trees and began pulsing. It seemed to be getting blacker as though gathering strength.

Jhona wasn't afraid of it, but she knew that it represented, or maybe it actually was, the dark energy Crullmar talked about. Then with a loud cracking sound, all the trees on that side of the meadow, the ones Jhona had flattened, all stood back up. As soon as that had happened, the dark shadow formed itself into a thin line of blackness that rose into the sky, piercing the overcast cloud.

It reminded her of a javelin thrown straight up. She got the distinct impression that if she didn't do something it would come back down like an arrow shot straight up into the sky. Jhona had no doubt that it would pierce her from head to toe. Straight through. She had to do something, but what?

I SHOT AN ARROW INTO THE AIR

"Circle," Jhona thought. She raised her hands and made a circle with her thumb and forefinger. She then jerked her hands apart just slightly.

This time a massive shockwave flew out in all directions. It passed through Jhona with no effect, but crossed the meadow in a flash, vaporizing all the snow and leaving black, scorched earth behind. As soon as it hit the tree line, there was a very heavy explosion, but one that made no noise at all. Jhona thought it was like an explosion in outer space where there is no air to transmit sound. She could feel it in her chest, though.

All of the trees as far as Jhona could see burst into flames. In the middle of the meadow, Jhona was in the center of a ring of fire so intense that she feared she might catch on fire herself.

The fire yielded a column of thick, black smoke. It was forming into a cylinder, but it had a polished surface. It began rising into the clouds surrounding the thin line of smoke that the opposing force had created.

Projected on the inside of the column, which was now a perfect black cylinder, Jhona could see herself sitting in the airline seat with Annabelle beside her. It was the Hologram projection again. Annabelle was shaking her and saying something to her. Jhona could see that the "fasten seat belt" sign was lit.

In that same instant the cylinder of smoke collapsed in on itself engulfing the thin spear of smoke made by the opposing dark energy. It produced another explosion, only this one was much stronger than the last one.

Blackness fell over Jhona like someone had thrown a blanket over her head. It was warm and felt safe, comfortable, like a down blanket on a cold morning when she had to get up and go to school. All she wanted to do was sleep a little longer. Sleep and think about that dream. It was just a dream, wasn't it, just a dream?

She began to hear what Annabelle was saying to her.

"Wake up, Jhona. You've got to fasten your seatbelt. We're making an emergency landing."

WINTER'S BEDS

Jhona came awake with a jolt. "What's going on, Annabelle?"

"They just announced some sort of mechanical problem, and we've got to land in Dallas."

"Dallas? We're only half way to New York."

"We'll find a connecting flight as soon as possible."

In times of emergency, the air traffic controllers can really show their "stuff." The very complex Dallas/Fort Worth air space was totally redirected to clear a safety cone that allowed Jhona's flight to transcend from 33,000 feet to a cleared runway in what seemed to the passengers to be just a few minutes.

After a safe landing, the jet was escorted to a gate in a very remote part of the airfield. All of the passengers were encouraged to quickly leave the airplane with their luggage. Airline staff began busily calculating various alternate flights for the off-boarded passengers.

Before jumping into that fray, Crullmar gathered everyone together and told them to hold still while he placed a call to Samantha Idaho. Jhona was clutching the bag containing the tape. She was tempted to just chuck it into the nearest garbage can. Instead, she decided not to think about it as she sat there listening to snatches of conversation among the other passengers.

She tuned in to a conversation between one of the passengers and a crewmember. The jest of that discussion was that a warning light came on indicating there was a fire on the right engine. A quick examination of that engine showed no indication of a fire and they were concluding that the warning light was faulty. Mechanics were working to replace the light and wiring, and would place the plane back in service as soon as repairs were completed.

Jhona thought to herself, *"Sure, back in service. There's no way in hell I'm getting back on that plane."*

Just as that thought crossed her mind, Crullmar walked up. "I just got off the phone with Samantha. She says we should stay over here in Dallas. She's going to catch the next flight she can get to Dallas. She thinks we've been taken here on purpose to further our quest."

"What quest is that?" Jhona asked. She didn't think she was on any kind of a quest for God's sake. What was she looking for, the Holy Grail?

"Jhona, Samantha has a lot of experience dealing with the kind of witchcraft involving talismans that are infused with dark energy. We think that's what the Ruby tape is. Sometimes if an object is created from circumstances involving extreme points of violence or other emotionally charged incidences, dark energy can be attracted to the object and can infuse it with elements of both dark matter and dark energy."

Peter, who had been listening to the conversation, spoke up. "That's what you said about the tape. That it was a kind of micro black hole or something."

"How did we get from a black hole to a quest?" Jeff asked.

Crullmar noticed several fellow passengers were beginning to listen to their conversation. "Look, guys, let's get to a hotel, and I'll explain this all in a bit more detail. We'll get settled in, and we'll have a conference as soon as Samantha arrives. Whatever our next move is, it's most likely they'll be happening here in Dallas.

"In fact, I think we should take rooms in the Hotel Texas in Fort Worth. That's the hotel the Kennedys stayed in on the eve the assassination. It just seems right for some reason."

"It sure as hell doesn't seem right to me," Jhona thought. *"But neither does anything else about this deal."*

SHE KEEPS HER VISIONS TO HERSELF

Jhona wasn't really listening to all that. She kept thinking about her *vision*. That's what it was, a kind of secret vision, something just between herself and another, what, entity? There was another force in that meadow for sure, and Jhona knew she had literally blown it away. And just with the slightest movement of her hands, too. Her power was nothing short of incredible. It would be difficult keeping it to herself.

She heard Crullmar mention the word, quest. Jhona didn't feel that she was on a quest of any sort. She was in a contest, an actual battle, a battle of strength, willpower, focus, and raw, supernatural power.

A quest is where you look for something. Jhona had already found it. The power. The incredible power, and she'd barely even used any of it at all. She could feel vast reserves of power that she could draw upon. It was all deep inside of her. Down where Dorothy had gone. It felt like a vast lake of black water—a lake with no bottom.

She even liked experimenting with it a bit. It didn't feel like a physical thing. It was definitely raw energy, kind of a dark mass that moved and undulated as she breathed. She knew it was where Dorothy had gone. They were no longer two separate entities. They were one now—one very, very powerful force.

She knew that force came from dark energy, but that didn't concern her. It was dark energy alright, but dark energy manifested and controlled by her Dorothy-self. Dark energy that her Jhona-self could focus and use like a weapon by projecting streams of dark matter wherever she wanted it. Dark matter, antimatter really, that would annihilate anything it touched.

Jhona was no longer concerned with the tape. She knew her power had initially come from the tape, but through Dorothy she had accumulated such immense reserves that the tape was just a minor part of it. *A powerful witch controls her talismans, not the other way around.* That thought was in her Dorothy-mind.

Jhona insisted on carrying the voodoo bag with the tape in it. She knew she didn't really need the bag, but she wasn't yet ready to reveal the truth of her strength to the others. She had become a different person, a different *kind* of person, a *dangerous* kind of person, perhaps, the most dangerous person in the entire universe. *Perhaps*…the most powerful person who had ever lived…*would* ever live, a goddess, really.

A very small smile spread slowly over her face. None of the others noticed. She would have to tell them about it at some point. Or maybe not…

I WANT TO TAKE YOU AWAY FROM ALL THIS

After checking into their respective rooms, everyone decided to take a nap since it was a couple of hours until dinner, and Samantha wasn't even scheduled to arrive until 4:30 that afternoon. Jhona surprised Peter by telling him that she wanted her own room.

"I just need some private time to unwind, Peter. After all we were almost in a plane crash."

"Plane crash?" Peter looked hurt. "It was just a malfunctioning warning light."

"Believe that if you want, Peter."

"Believe that if I want? What…"

It was too late to reason with her. She was already heading to the elevator. Peter turned to Jeff.

"Well, okay then. Jeff, I guess we could get a room together."

"Sure, Dude. We can do that," Jeff said, somewhat absentmindedly, as he watched Jhona disappear into the crowded elevator.

"I wish I knew what is bugging her."

"Dude, like you can't figure *that* out? Let's see, whatever could it be? Hummmm. I know. How about she was almost killed in a fire? Or maybe she's having weird experiences that she doesn't understand? Maybe that's it. What do you think?"

"I think it's more that she is having weird experiences that she perfectly well *does* understand. That's what has me freaked out, Dude."

"Boys, let's not let this get to us any more than it already has," said Crullmar. I think it's quite appropriate that she is taking some time to herself, but I don't really think she should be left alone, especially with that talisman.

"Annabelle, why don't you go up and have a talk with her. Actually, see if you can talk her into sharing her room with you. I don't think she should be alone."

"I agree with that," Annabelle said. "You know that false alarm was created by Jhona. I looked over at her right before the alarm went off, and she was trembling all over. I think she was having another astral projection."

"No doubt. No doubt," said Crullmar. "I think we'll be able to control it better once Samantha gets here. I'll prepare my room for a coven, and let's meet back down here for dinner at five. Samantha should be checking in about the time we finish."

"Alright, and we'll be able to see how the little "fire panic" will be handled by the TV news," said Annabelle.

DO YOU SEE THEM? THEY'RE ALL AROUND

Jhona was sitting on her bed just staring at the crazy patterns on the carpet when she heard the soft knock on her door. Her first thought was that Peter had come up to get some reassurance that she still loved him and all that crap. Jhona was feeling a lot of things, but love just wasn't one of them right now, at least not for Peter. He was just kind of there, that's all. Well, she was kind of glad he was there, she guessed. He was a dolt, but he was faithful. That counted for something.

The soft knock again.

What was she even doing here? Crullmar said that they were brought to Dallas on purpose. Jhona didn't like the idea of being *brought* someplace.

The soft knock again followed by Annabelle's voice, "Jhona."

Annabelle. Yes, she was cool. Jhona was beginning to feel that she could be trusted. It would be nice to talk to her. Jhona could hear the door being tried and then opened.

"Jhona. Is anything the matter? Are you okay?"

Jhona looked up from the carpet patterns. Her eyes were frightfully dilated. Like two black tunnels. The bag with the tape in it was sitting on her lap, her hands clutching the strap so hard that they were white.

"Annabelle. Hi. I was just looking…um…at the…carpet. It's so…interesting, like a Hologram. I can see things in it. Can you see things in it, Annabelle? I'll bet you can if you just look…"

Annabelle crossed the room and sat down next to her. She placed her hands on Jhona's. They felt terribly cold clutching the bag, her nails digging into the strap.

"Jhona. Let it go. Let the bag go for now."

Jhona looked up at Annabelle with those eyes. Eyes like two black holes, but she relaxed her grip a bit.

"That's right, Jhona. Just let it go. You'll be alright."

Jhona let go of the strap. The bag slid off her lap and hit the floor with a thump. As it hit the carpet, ripples moved out from the bag as though a large rock had been tossed into a still pond.

"See that, Annabelle? See the ripples? Do you know what that means?"

Annabelle was becoming frightened. The ripples moved across the room hitting chair legs, the desk, the trashcan, the bed frame, and anything else on the floor. Each time one of those objects was hit, other ripples began moving across the room creating interference patterns.

"N-no," she said. Her eyes were transfixed on the interference patterns. It was a bit like looking through a kaleidoscope. None of the patterns made any sense, but they kept moving—bouncing off each other.

"Jhona, look beyond the patterns. Look through them. I'll help you." Annabelle placed her hand on the back of Jhona's neck. Jhona felt a warm sensation moving through her neck and into her body. It felt safe.

Annabelle began getting visions, one right after another in rapid sequence. Suddenly, she saw Dorothy lying on her deathbed.

"Jhona. Do you see Dorothy?" Jhona nodded her head. "She's going to help you, Jhona. Let her do it."

Now Jhona could see pictures made by the interference patterns. They looked like Holograms, like that scene from Star Wars, kind of transparent but three-dimensional. There was Dorothy lying on her bed. She slowly raised her hand. It was black.

Jhona looked down at her own hand. The one Dorothy had entered in the meadow. It was pitch black, too, but it felt warm, warm and powerful. More power than she had ever felt before.

"Now, Jhona. Point your palm at the Hologram. Let your mind open to what you see. Just let the visions come."

Jhona shook her head. She was becoming afraid. Her body began shaking all over. "No. No. Please. No."

"It's okay, Jhona. You're safe right now. Let the power protect you. Look for the other talisman."

"Other ta-talisman? What other talisman? I don't understand. Please let me come back."

"No, Jhona. You must find the other talisman. That's the only way to be safe."

"Okay." As Jhona raised her hand, the vision of Dorothy on her deathbed raised her arm, too. Open circles that looked like large bracelets made of colorful smoke flowed from Dorothy's arm and circled Jhona's hand turning it to tar black. Then her hand began turning to a glowing red, like a hot iron. Finally it turned white and a powerful shockwave blasted from Jhona's hand into the Hologram. A clap of thunder followed, echoing through the canyons of the city before fading out.

The Hologram instantly changed.

THE COLORS ARE EVERYWHERE

Samantha was rolling her bag through the hotel's revolving door when she heard the thunderclap. It was so loud that it made her lose her grip on the bag, and it clattered to the floor wedging itself into the revolving door. Samantha had no idea what could have caused the noise, and she expected everyone in the lobby to be startled as well, but everyone just went on doing what they were before the sound. *Didn't they hear it?*

Samantha became aware of the people stuck in the door shouting encouragement at her to move the bag. At least they were more polite about it than New Yorkers would have been.

As she got the bag unstuck, she realized that the sound must have something to do with Crullmar and his sister. *Were they really conjuring without waiting for her? And that noise…*

As she was making her way to the check-in counter, Crullmar spotted her and waived her over to their table in the lobby restaurant.

"Hello, Sam…" Crullmar started to say.

"Joe. What is going on? Didn't you hear that clap of thunder?"

"What? What clap of thunder? You heard a clap of thunder?"

"Are you guys conjuring without waiting for me?"

"Well, not that I know about, I mean Annabelle is upstairs with Jhona, but…"

"Joe. Something is going on up there. Would you please go see what it is while I check in?"

"Okay. Boys, please introduce yourselves to Samantha here. I'll be back in a few minutes."

The elevator seemed to take forever getting to Jhona's floor, but finally the doors opened and Crullmar knocked gently on the door. With no response, he tried the knob and the door opened. Moving into the room, he could see Jhona and Annabelle sitting together on the edge of the bed staring at something on the floor. Jhona's hand was outstretched and appeared to be white hot.

As he moved closer to the pair he began to make out what they were staring at.

It was a moving Hologram of Jack Ruby in the basement of the Dallas Police Department. It showed him approaching Oswald as the officers who were escorting Oswald looked everywhere but in the direction Ruby was coming from. Ruby got so close to Oswald that he could have punched him in the face. Instead he pushed the gun to within an inch or two of Oswald's stomach and jerked the trigger.

The officers holding onto Oswald's arms looked incredulous, as though it never occurred to them that an assassination attempt could be made on the most hated man in the country.

The Hologram instantly changed to that of the bullet as it smashed through Oswald's stomach and several other internal organs. Each time it hit an organ it created a sickening splash of blood. Finally the bullet came to rest, and it was over.

Jhona's arm began returning to its natural color as she lowered it onto her lap. The interference patterns played out, and she stood up and went into the bathroom and closed the door. Sounds of Jhona's retching could be heard through the closed door.

"What's going on, Ann?" Crullmar asked.

"She's beginning to see the texture of the Holographic universe. Dorothy's essence is acting as a kind of guide. She's become allied with her—completely bonded in spirit. In essence, Dorothy is teaching Jhona how to become an effective witch. In life, Dorothy had insight, but lacked strength. Jhona is frighteningly powerful and is gaining Dorothy's insight as well."

"I see," said Crullmar. Actually, he didn't have a clue about how this could have happened. Jhona was just a normal girl. How could she have gathered all this power and learned to control it in just a few days?

"Samantha's here now. Downstairs. I think we should have her come up and listen to what Jhona has to say about this latest excursion into the Hologram. This time she actually reached the other side of it."

"Just be aware that there is an adversary at work, someone or something that has another talisman and wants to combine it with Jhona's tape. I think *it* is very much afraid of Jhona's growing power. If Jhona learns how to effectively manipulate the underlying interference waves of the Holographic base of the universe, nothing will be able to stop her."

"Okay. I'll Give Jhona another ten minutes and then bring everyone up."

LET'S MAKE IT A TRUE DAILY DOUBLE, AJAX

Thinking that it would be best if everyone could relax over dinner, but knowing that they needed privacy, Doctor Crullmar took food orders and called room service. They all spent the next hour in Crullmar's suite getting to know each other a little better. Everyone avoided talking about the visions.

At six o'clock they tuned the television to the local news channel and watched the story of their emergency landing.

Since there was no damage to the airplane and no one was hurt, the story was only given sixty seconds of air time about half way through the broadcast. After the story was finished, Crullmar turned off the TV.

"Okay people. This is a good place to bring Samantha up to speed on what's been going on with Jhona—and the rest of us.

"Samantha, this all started when Jhona, Peter and Jeff received a box from Jhona's grandfather. The box was filled with personal items once owned by Dorothy Kilgallen. Dorothy was a well-known New York columnist and television personality."

"Yes, I know," said Samantha. "It was called *What's My Line?*".

"That's right, Sam. Grandpa's father, Jhona's great-grandfather, had been Dorothy's attorney. Back in '65, Dorothy was found dead under mysterious circumstances in her townhouse. The box and its contents were placed in great-grandpa's trust. Grandpa was retiring and cleaning out his office when the box was discovered in the back of a little-used storage room.

"Grandpa shipped the box to his trusted grand-daughter to provide an inventory of its contents. This inventory was to be presented to Dorothy's heirs who would be able to decide what to do with them. The heirs instructed grandpa to dispose of all of it, which Jhona, Peter and Jeff did—except for one item—a tape recording of the last known interview with Jack Ruby. An interview conducted in private by Dorothy. Just Dorothy and Ruby were in the room.

"This tape has never been heard by anyone except Dorothy, and now the four of us. After making it, Dorothy stated that she had enough information to blow the JFK conspiracy wide open. What she had was the tape, so she must have been referring to it."

"And now we have it," said Samatha.

"And now we have it. Over there on that nightstand in that voodoo bag, but what is it, Sam?" asked Crullmar.

"I'm guessing you have your theories, Joe."

"We have theories and some pretty startling experiences to go with them."

"I can probably guess, but go ahead. Let's hear them." Jhona began squirming in her chair.

"Relax, Jhona. It'll be alright," said Crullmar.

Jhona related all of the visions she had experienced since the initial levitation. She left out the intense sex she had with Peter.

Crullmar continued, "I think it's about as clear as anything gets that the little roll of tape is a very powerful talisman. A talisman that can project our friend, Jhona, here into the actual interference patterns that makes up our Holographic universe. With the talisman, Jhona, here, can not only visit the alternate universes that course all around us, but it has given her incredible powers to actually modify any or all of those universes...including our own.

"Jhona, I'd like to let Sam, er, Samantha tell you what a talisman is, and why it has been affecting you the way it has."

"Okay, Joe. Jhona, a talisman can be made out of any object. It can be created by a person, say a witch or someone with developed, oh, you could call them

190

supernatural skill sets. Mostly, however, they are objects that have been involved in very intense situations, or happenings, vortices of intense emotions, like tragedies. The objects absorb the interference patterns of the Holograms created by those occurrences.

"Most people will touch such an object and not really feel anything…maybe just a sense of wonder or something. Think about the objects that have been brought up from the Titanic shipwreck. Touching a tile or a watch from the wreckage might create a small sense of tragedy in most people, or maybe they would get an indistinct image from the wreck. Only a select few of them would ever see as deeply into the tragedy as Jhona. Jhona has the natural gift to see the Holographic patterns. The talisman, Dorothy's interview tape, gives her great personal power as well.

"Actually, all of the objects involved in the JFK assassination and aftermath are very powerful talismans," said Crullmar. "Fortunately, most of them, actually pretty much all of them, are locked up in the government archives—the rifle Oswald used, all the bullets fired into the president, Jackie's pink dress, the roses she was holding, and just about every other object from that event.

"A few have ended up with people who like to collect weird objects. I know that Ruby's pistol was purchased by an anonymous gun collector. That would be an incredibly powerful talisman, but I'm betting that collector has no idea of its power.

"Now we have the tape. It's a bit like holding onto a hot potato. It sends out patterns to the Holographic network that can be picked up by witches and other psychically sensitive people. What I'm thinking is that another talisman is in the hands of someone who wants all the power he or she can accumulate. That talisman is helping that person hone in on ours, and challenge Jhona. We're going to need to find out, if we can, who that person is and the identity of his or her talisman. That's why Samantha is here today. Sam, would you like to take it from here?"

SAM TAKES IT FROM THERE

"There are a couple of things that seem obvious to me. First, I believe we were diverted here to Dallas by some aspect of the tape. What we need to find is here, not in New York. That makes sense because Dallas is where the events took place. There is a lot of residual energy at each of the locations, the plaza, the grassy knoll, all of that. For us, it's likely to be the basement of the Dallas Police Department.

"The second thing is, I think you, Peter and Jeff, encountered this…ah, rival."

"Encountered him?" asked Jeff. "When would that have happened?"

"It's obvious when you think about it," said Samantha. "Remember when you went to that library to play the tape? That assistant who escorted you to the media room, and then hung around?"

"Yes," said Peter.

"Did he look anything like this person?" Samantha held up a close-up photo of Oswald's face.

"Dude, that's *him.* You mean Oswald was actually…how come we didn't recognize…"

"Because that recognition was blocked by the Oswald entity. What happened when you went back to the library?"

"Yeah," said Peter. "No room. No librarian. No assistant. Just a brick wall."

"Just a brick wall," said Samantha. "A brick wall. I don't know about the librarian, but the assistant was probably some form of Oswald.

"It may not have been the actual essence of Oswald. It could have been any skillful witch using Oswald's power—kind of like Jhona is using Dorothy's."

"I'm not using anyone's *power,*" said Jhona. "I'm using *my* power. Dorothy is just helping to guide me.

That's all. We don't share power. It's all mine, and it's so vast that no little fucking twerp like that asshole, Oswald, could even come close to it."

Everyone stared at Jhona, taken aback by her outburst.

"What? Does that surprise you? What do you think you're dealing with? Why do you think the Oswald guy retreats every time he tries confronting me? He runs away like a puppy with his tail between his legs. It's actually funny. I've got to go take a shit. You guys just keep having your little conversation. Figure it out as best you can."

Jhona retreated to the bathroom and slammed the door.

GETTING A HANDLE ON THINGS

After an embarrassing silence, Samantha continued.

"You may not have actually been in a library. That's the power of whatever talisman they have. And Jhona, think about the confrontations she's been having, the visions we've been calling them. Well, they're not visions. They're full blown confrontations, confrontations taking place at the very edge of the Hologram. The edge of sanity."

The toilet flushed, water ran in the sink, and Jhona emerged. She picked up the voodoo bag and began casually swinging it, one finger in the strap.

"So what do you suggest we do, then?" Jhona held up the bag and looked at them.

"We're going to use the talisman we've got to go on the offensive.

"What does that mean, Samantha?" Figuring it meant that she, Jhona, was going to have to do something scary, she was getting concerned. She had developed a lot of self-confidence since Dorothy entered her, but there was a black edge of fear surrounding the whole thing. Her newly found bravado had helped keep it at bay.

"We're going to send you back into the Hologram. Into the actual Holographic plate, where the interference patterns for our universe are generated. This time we're going to actively protect you with a coven," said Samantha.

"Even I know a coven means a circle of witches. Not only do we not have any witches here, but also there are only six of us. How can that make a coven?"

"We can make an effective coven with as few as three people, and they don't all have to be witches. I'm a witch, Annabelle is a witch, and now, Jhona, you're a witch. In fact, even though you are unaware of it, you have become a very, very powerful witch, even more so by your bonding with Dorothy."

"Unaware of it? You think I'm unaware of that? Have you not been listening to me? I know how powerful I am now, but that doesn't mean I'm anxious to return to that interference place," said Jhona.

"It'll be okay, Jhona. Let Dorothy guide you. She's both inside you and behind the Holographic plate. She'll be watching the interference patterns, and she'll be able to see anything being manifested to harm you. Listen to her while you are inside the Hologram. Meanwhile, we'll be blocking threats to you outside the plate."

"Inside the Hologram? I'm supposed to go *inside* the Hologram? I don't even know what the Hologram is. How do I go inside it, and more importantly, how do I get back *outside* of it?"

"Dorothy. Dorothy will help you find the way back. Just don't lose track of her, and you'll be fine."

"Well, okay, if it will stop all this nonsense. What am I supposed to be looking for behind this Hologram plate, or whatever it is?"

"You're looking for an object of power, what we call a talisman," said Crullmar. "We don't know what it is, but we do know it has something to do with Ruby shooting Oswald. There's some object floating around that is connected with that event. That's why we were redirected here to Dallas/Fort Worth, and that's why the Hologram showed the actual shooting."

"Let me walk you through how the coven will work, Jhona," said Samantha. Out of her bag she took what looked like a fat stack of cardboard squares and began placing them on the carpet. When completed, the squares created a protective magic circle with all kinds of strange symbols scattered throughout the circle. She pulled out a small compass.

"Okay, Jhona, you'll sit in the middle here, and we'll place Peter, Jeff, and Joe at the cardinal points; Peter at the east, Jeff at the west, and Joe at the south. I'll sit at the north. We'll act as the guardians of the gates. We'll protect you from intruders, and the circle will seal you off inside the Hologram. You'll be safe from dark energy but able to move freely throughout the Hologram. Just let Dorothy guide you.

"I'm going to say some incantations now, so why don't you go sit on the couch with Joe and he'll explain a little more about what the Holographic universe is and how you will be able to manipulate it.

"First, I want each of you to fill up a glass with water and set them down next to me. I'm going to purify them. Once I've done that everyone is to drink one of them in as few swallows as possible—without choking."

THE GAG REFLEX

Having experienced much of the Hologram first hand, Jhona was very quick to comprehend Crullmar's lecture. Meanwhile, Samantha spent the next half hour moving around the magic circle adding symbols and pouring little piles of herbs and powders onto various spots. The whole time she was mumbling incoherent poems or incantations.

Jhona glanced at her occasionally and thought she looked ridiculous. How could a cardboard circle with little piles of what looked like lint from a vacuum cleaner possibly keep her safe? She had been inside that so-called Hologram, and it was a dangerous place. Somehow, though, Jhona knew she was up to the task. She even realized that whenever Samantha completed a little pile of dirt, or salt, or whatever it was, she could feel a minor shock wave enter her body from her "Dorothy hand."

She realized her arm was sticking straight out and following Samantha as she moved around the circle. The shocks were little circular sparks of different colors that moved up her arm like oversized bracelets. The actual shocks came as each ring hit her shoulder and thumped into her body. Each time she shuddered a little as a strong sense of warmth coursed through her body.

Finally, when Samantha announced the circle was ready, Jhona's body was actually pulsing with anticipation.

"Jhona," Samantha said, "If you have to use your power to manipulate the interference patterns, make sure you do it through your right hand. That way Dorothy can help you maximize your strength. When you do this, keep your left hand hidden. You will be holding the tape in that hand. That's your talisman and the focus of much of your power. Make a tight fist with it. It will contain both your power from the talisman and your weakness, which is your fear. If your fingers become visible, you are open to invasion. Got it?"

Jhona stood up. She felt like she was as tall as the Statue of Liberty and made out of stone—living, pulsing stone. She made a fist with her left hand, grabbing the tape and burying it into the folds of her robe. *When did she put on a robe?* she wondered.

"Step into the circle now, Jhona," Samantha ordered.

Jhona looked down at the floor. It seemed to be miles away. She could see the tiny faces of the others tilted upward and looking at her. They were so far away, so tiny. She was so massive.

She lifted her giant right foot and moved it over the faces to just above the circle. It was a Statue of Liberty foot, sandal and all, and it was huge.

Gently she lowered it until it covered the circle and all the people. She was afraid of crushing them, but…she was also pleased with the knowledge that she could crush them if she wanted.

"You're doing fine, Jhona." Samantha's voice drifted up to her from so very far away.

"Now gently lower your foot and bring the other one into the circle."

Jhona lowered her giant foot until it touched the floor, or whatever it was touching. Floor didn't seem to be the right word. It was some sort of a surface, but spongy, not solid.

"Okay. Bring your other foot into the circle."

Jhona put all of her massive weight onto her right foot and lifted her left one. As she lifted it the circle began expanding, but when she looked down at her foot she was shocked to see that it wasn't a foot at all. It was a giant hoof.

YOU ARE LOST AND GONE FOREVER

Jhona hesitated as she stared down at her leg. It was a goat's leg, all covered in black wool with a black, shiny goat's hoof where her foot should have been. She just stared at it.

"Jhona. Jhona. Listen to me. Jhona."

Jhona was beginning to feel panic. The leg didn't feel warm and powerful, as did the rest of her body. It was more of a cold, prickly sensation, and it was moving up. It was right near her crotch. "Samantha," she yelled. The voice boomed through the canyons just as the blast had earlier. It created overlapping echoes that came back to her. Each echo hit her like a blow from a boxer.

"Listen to me, Jhona. Keep moving your foot into the circle. Do you hear me? Don't stop moving your foot."

The circle was pulsing as though it were impatiently waiting to enclose Jhona's foot. Waiting for her to move. Finally, in a wave of desperation she completed the move and her foot instantly changed back into the Statue of Liberty foot.

As she gently lowered it, the circle coursed upward making a glowing cylinder that encased her. Her self-confidence returned, but there was just a tinge of uncertainty.

"What happened?" her voice boomed out like a giant foghorn, but there was no answer from the circle.

She heard a voice in her head. It was less like a voice…more like little silver bells tinkling.

"Look up, Jhona. Look up."

It was Dorothy. She was standing, no, not standing, but floating just outside the glowing cylinder. She was so beautiful, full of intelligence, a beautiful mind, a bright mind. Jhona could see the brightness. It looked like a halo.

Dorothy raised her arm. Jhona raised hers and as their fingers met they were melded into one being, a being of silver and ice. Of waves of power and eddies of gentleness. Of dawns and sunsets melded into one glorious golden hue. In spite of the melding, Jhona still retained her sense of self…her identity of being Jhona, but that self was melded with an incredible power/gentleness, and she began floating down a long hallway. It reminded her of being in a little boat and bobbing into the tunnel of love with Peter.

The hallway was like an art gallery. On either side were Holograms of various scenes. Some were little more than colors and fantastic shapes. Others were scenes from the Kennedys' lives. Some were scenes from Oswald's life: his first kiss with his wife, Marina; the birth of his daughter; posing with his rifle and pistol; wrapping the rifle in brown paper and getting a ride to work with his coworker.

"What's in the bag?" asked the coworker, a look of concern passing over his face.

"Just curtain rods," Oswald answered.

A moment of indecision passed again over the coworker's face. *"Curtain rods? Curtain rods that you are bringing to work? That makes no sense,"* he said to himself.

Another voice seemed to answer, a reassuring voice. *"Just curtain rods, though. Nothing dangerous, nothing to be worried about. Just curtain rods. That's all."* It was a voice inside the coworker's head, a voice of reason, an external voice, but a voice of reason none-the-less. The car rolled into the parking lot behind the Texas Schoolbook Depository.

"You want to leave those in the car?" asked the coworker, hoping for a reason he didn't fully understand that the answer would be yes.

"Nah," Oswald replied. "Better take them inside."

"Okay," said the coworker, "Makes sense."

Even though it didn't. It didn't make any goddamn sense at all, Jhona thought. But no one thinks *gun, assassination.* No one ever thinks that. *No one.* The image faded. Jhona-Dorothy continued drifting down the hall.

There were plenty of other images; some of the Kennedys, Jack arguing with Jackie about coming down to the breakfast. It was *that* morning. Jackie said she didn't want to. Wasn't up to it. Jack insisted. There was some shouting, but it ended quickly. They were a political couple, a practical couple. They understood how to maintain the proper image. The image everyone wanted to believe. Desperately needed to believe.

Jackie knew she would have to do what he wanted eventually.

He kept leaving to go downstairs. Had to give a speech. No one cared. They wanted Jackie. "Where's your lovely wife?" Governor Connelly smiles, his wife sitting next to him all proper, a dutiful politician's wife.

Jack took the podium again. It was so early in the morning in Fort Worth. Had to drive to Dallas in a damn convertible. It was cold, too. "You know how women are," he said.

That got a knowing laugh from everyone. Even the dutiful wives. Everyone loved Jackie. *"If they only knew what a pain in the ass she could be,"* he thought. What a pain in the ass she *was* being this morning. A morning filled with Jackie fussing. Jackie fears. She was always afraid for Jack, but more so this morning than usual. She hated Texas. Hated having to be there. Hated sitting in the back of a convertible surrounded by strangers. Surrounded by Texans.

"Jack, there's something skimming the shadows, something bad."

He couldn't console her. "Put on the pink outfit," he said before leaving for the third time that morning. "You look best in it." He thought of Marilyn. She looked best in nothing at all. It was a bad thought. He knew it. She was gone now. Was it really his fault? He never promised her anything. She knew the score. So did Jackie. Better than Marilyn, actually. Why were the most beautiful women the most difficult?

"Come down as soon as you can. Everyone loves you." He hesitated for a heartbeat, "I love you."

She turned up her face to receive a kiss. She felt a wave of fear that it might be the last one. It was hurried. Impatient. Sad. She touched her lips as he left. She grabbed the pink outfit. The door closed.

Later someone handed her a bouquet of roses, beautiful red ones. "*Like blood*," she thought for a moment.

ENDINGS

The number of Holograms on the walls increased, some showing only a still image of something. A single, private thought reflected in a face, *Secret Servicemen looking at...what?* There were windows and crowds of people on all sides.

The caravan moved slowly. Giving everyone a good look. Smiles. Sunshine. One rifle. Maybe more. Who could really say? Slowing even more for the turn into Dealey Plaza.

The hallway ended. Jhona-Dorothy floated into a room, a focal point of fate. Oswald was ready, as ready as anyone has ever been, alone in the sixth floor room, controlling his breathing, thinking he might get one, or at the most two shots. Crisp. Clear. Precise.

Aiming. Back of the head. The ultimate sniper target. Car moving slowly away. Squeezing. Good training. Government training. Marine training. Nothing mattered but the squeezing.

Sound of the shot was deafening. Cracks appeared in the Holographic plate. Two more shots in rapid succession. Who shoots like that? That accurately? At a moving target?

The plate shattered. Each piece containing the whole scene. Scattered across the floor.

Indecision now. What to do? He didn't know. So sure of everything, Oswald now felt confused. There were thousands of Oswalds scattered across the floor, each one alone, totally alone. People wanted him now. Dangerous people.

Hadn't thought beyond the shots. They were over. Now what?

Jhona became aware of a presence out in the hall. She felt Dorothy tighten up. Gripping their conjoined hands. Dorothy was scared, but brave.

Jhona heard the bell-words again. "The hallway." She found that she could kind of will herself to drift out there again. She could see a door way down at the end. It was just slightly opened, and a bright light spilled into the hallway. She could see a figure, Man? Woman? She wasn't sure. Someone dressed in black, completely head to toe, except the toes weren't toes, they were hooves.

ESCUSE ME WHILE I KISS THE SKY

A flash of blue light flew down the hall smashing into the Jhona-Dorothy. As it hit, the cylinder surrounding the Jhona-Dorothy lit up for a second, and the Jhona-Dorothy could see the four guardians surrounding them take a blow. The Jhona-Dorothy felt nothing, but the cylinder flexed and got darker for a moment.

"Your hand, Jhona. Protect your hand."

The Jhona-Dorothy looked down and saw the naked left hand. She/it quickly put it in the folds of the robes. The Jhona-Dorothy looked up. There was an angry expression on the Jhona-Dorothy face. The face was a Hologram that looked a lot like a tiger's face. Teeth were bared in a menacing growl, and then the face separated from the Jhona-Dorothy and sped down the hall, heading right for the doorway. The entire hallway was filled with a howling fury. The door closed the instant the face hit it.

The door couldn't contain the force of the Jhona-Dorothy. It completely blew apart like an over inflated balloon.

They were outside on a plane. It seemed to stretch forever in all directions. It was pitch black, but the sky thing above was glowing, casting a dim light over the entire scene.

The Jhona-Dorothy had transformed from a giant stone statue into a hateful creature that looked something like a lion with spikes covering every inch of its body. It walked upright, yet had only three legs. The left foreleg was hidden in a dense thicket of thorns, which grew out of its side. The right foreleg was black with glowing, red talons, ready to rip.

It could see the goat-form speeding away. The Jhona-Dorothy was furious. It felt only two things, an immense flowing of power, and a hateful desire to bring down the fleeing goat-thing. It crouched down low on its back legs and made a powerful, soaring leap in the direction the goat-thing was moving.

The Jhona-Dorothy was consumed with a desire for blood. It wanted nothing else but to rip the goat-thing apart and feel its bones being crushed, shattered between its teeth. It would use its back claws to dig out the goat-thing's bowels and then fling them to the horizon. It roared again shaking its head back and forth in pure, unbridled fury.

Thick strands of saliva were projected from the thing's mouth and landed on the plate. As each piece of slimy matter landed, crazy interference patterns shot across the plate's surface. The patterns generated intense Holograms of various scenes of the JFK assassination, which attained a blinding brightness before dimming back into nothingness.

As it landed on the goat-thing, there was nothing there, except the surface of the Holographic plate. The Jhona-Dorothy creature looked down at the interference pattern it had made on the plate as it landed. The interference patterns generated a Hologram of the goat-thing just inside the surface. The two creatures were eye-to-eye, less than three inches apart, but separated by the glass-like Holographic universe.

The goat-thing laughed as it held up something in its fist. The fist slowly opened as the Jhona-Dorothy felt a paralysis set in. It could only watch as an object was revealed nesting in the coal blackness of the goat-thing's sinewy hand.

HELL HATH NO FURY

Slowly the object came into view as the black hand opened. It was small, about the size of the tip of a little finger, and it had a dull shine to it. It was a bullet, one that had been fired. The Jhona-Dorothy knew that because of some television crime show Jhona had watched in the distant past. Lands and groves had been pressed into the copper sheathing. The bullet was just slightly deformed with the tip slightly flattened. There were also a few pieces missing.

The other talisman, it had to be. Just as that thought had passed through the Jhona-Dorothy's mind, the goat-thing began making a mean, throaty laugh. It shoved the bullet right up against the glass surface that made up the Holographic plate.

"Want it?" came a raspy voice that sounded as though it originated in the throat of a partially decomposed corpse.

As the bullet struck the inner surface of the plate an intense Hologram was pushed through the *glass*. First it showed Ruby thrusting his pistol at Oswald, and then the gun went off with a boom that was so loud it caused the entire plate to vibrate as though struck by an earthquake.

The Hologram followed the bullet as it entered Oswald's chest. The bullet's path was rendered in slow motion, and illuminated. Not with light, but with more of an understanding of what was happening as it drilled through various vital organs. It smashed against Oswald's spine or maybe the bottom part of a rib, spun around and came to rest just below the skin of his back. A few pieces flew off the bullet and exited his back in several places.

The Hologram ended by turning the plate back into opaque blackness. The Jhona-Dorothy was panting, exhausted. It could hear dim voices way off in a distance somewhere, calling. It just wanted to sleep, but the voices were insistent and unyielding.

"Jhona," they called weakly. "Jhona, bring out your talisman and follow it back."

What talisman? What were the voices talking about?

"...in your left hand. Bring out the talisman in your left hand."

Left hand? Jhona didn't have a left hand. She looked down. Her left arm disappeared into the folds of her robe. She was able to pull her hand out of the robe. Her hand was squeezing the tape. Squeezing it so hard that it made her hand hurt. She tried releasing her grip, but each time she gripped the tape harder.

And then the tape began to heat up. It felt red-hot. Jhona had to release it. She threw it away from herself as hard as she could, but it didn't fly away as she expected it would. Instead, it circled her making a vortex that began sucking her down.

She was spinning, getting sick to her stomach, just like when she was on that teacup ride at Disneyland. She began vomiting. Someone had a grip on her arm and someone else had a hand on her back.

"That's it, Jhona," someone said. "Get it all out. It's alright." It was Samantha. Jhona looked into her blue eyes. Jhona hadn't noticed the wrinkles around Samantha's eyes, and she began wondering how old she was.

"Can you talk, Jhona?" Samantha asked. "What did you see?"

Jhona kept her gaze on Samantha's wrinkled eyes. They seemed kind, concerned. But they were very, very wrinkled. It made her think of Dorothy's eyes. Weren't they wrinkled, too? She tried to remember, but her head hurt.

"Jhona, what did you see?" Again, the questions. Jhona just wanted to sleep now.

"Jhona," It was Samantha again. Why did she want to know what…and then it came back to her. "The talisman," Jhona said. "It's the bullet, the one that Ruby fired into Oswald. That's the talisman, and it's far, far more powerful than the tape."

Samantha's kind hands guided her to the couch and helped her lay down. She gently opened Jhona's fingers, which were still gripping the tape. Jhona struggled for a brief moment, but then released her grip. Samantha quickly passed the tape to Annabelle who inserted it into the voodoo bag and placed it on the coffee table. It was hot to the touch.

Samantha removed the coverlet from one of the beds and threw it over Jhona. She began snoring happily.

IF YOU GO INTO THE WOODS

"Let's go into the other room and have a brief conference while Jhona gets some much needed rest," said Crullmar.

They all gathered in the attached bedroom and closed the door.

"My first question is about the shock wave we all felt. Is everyone okay?"

Jeff spoke up first. "I have a headache, but other than that I'm okay. That impact, or whatever it was, damn near took the breath right out of me."

Everyone agreed they felt the same.

"It just proves that setting up the guardians was a smart thing to do," said Samantha. "They were able to absorb the bulk of the shock along with the protective cylinder. It enabled Jhona to carry on the attack without hesitating."

Peter just shook his head and stared at the floor. "Dude, I just don't know. How much danger was Jhona in anyway? That was the freakiest experience I've ever had, and I've had a couple of heavy ones over the past few days."

"That's why we brought in Sam," said Annabelle. "She knows how to protect Jhona."

"But what is going on when Jhona enters that circle? What is she seeing? What is she experiencing? The whole thing just seems out of control if you ask me."

"We're not out of control, Peter," said Samantha. "Jhona is extremely powerful now—even without the talisman. She's learning how to face threats and how to manipulate the Holographic plate. With that knowledge there's really nothing she can't do."

"What do you mean, there's really nothing she can't do?" asked Jeff. "She's still just a girl. A girl facing some sort of destructive dark force—in a whole other dimension, or something."

"What I mean, Jeff, is that Jhona now has the power to manipulate reality. To form it into whatever serves her best like it's some kind of Play-Doh or something. I've never known anyone to achieve that degree of power.

"Who, or whatever, is challenging her when she enters that realm is clearly outclassed," said Annabelle.

"Yes, they're outclassed at the moment," added Samantha. "But, now they know about the other talisman—the bullet. If they get hold of that, things are going to even up quite a lot. With that one, they may even become more powerful than Jhona…much more powerful."

"So, what do we do next, Sam?" asked Crullmar. "Should we try to identify our foes, so to speak?"

"Of course it would help to know who we are up against, but it would be difficult for Jhona to ferret them out."

"What do you mean, Sam?" asked Crullmar.

"Well, as Jhona's guide, I was able to see what was happening to her. I could see through her third eye."

"A third eye?" said Peter. "What are you talking about? What's a third eye?"

"Jhona has developed a psychic vision that allows her to see the Holographic planes. It also allows me to kind of 'tap into' it and share her vision. I can also feel what she's feeling. That's how I know how strong she is getting.

"The reason I'm saying it would be hard for her to track down the, let's call it the opposition, is by how it behaved when Jhona attacked.

"It knew it wasn't nearly strong enough to meet the challenge head on, so it evaded her. Not only that, but it did it in such a way that its powers of evasion are nearly equal to Jhona's powers of brute strength. These two opponents are very well matched right now, but if Jhona ever gets hold of it, well, we'll see some real fireworks."

"So we can't go searching for the opponent. Are they searching for us?" asked Jeff.

"Well, Jeff, that's the crux of it. What is the other side doing?" asked Crullmar.

"I think they're doing exactly what we should do next," said Samantha. "They're trying to find the other talisman. The bullet that killed Oswald."

VISCOSITY

"Look, Doctor, I think there's something else we're forgetting," said Annabelle. "Why were we diverted here to Dallas?"

"No, I haven't forgotten that little fact. In fact I've been giving it a lot of thought. Dallas is certainly the focal point for all the negative energy projected into the Hologram. Two people were killed here—the two key people in this whole mess.

"It's likely there are a lot of residual interference patterns from those events. I think we're being guided...."

"Guided by who, I mean whom?" asked Jeff, correcting himself.

"Well, that's a hard question to answer, Jeff, but thinking about the talisman we possess, the tape, and the talisman we don't possess, the bullet. If I had to guess I'd say we've stumbled onto a conflict between the residual energy between two old foes. It's been going on for a long time."

"Two old foes?" asked Peter. "What old foes?"

"Oswald and Ruby."

"Oswald and Ruby?" said Peter. "What? They've both been dead like, forever."

"I know, Peter, but sometimes negative energy doesn't just disappear. It can actually feed upon itself. The more negative, the more dark energy it can draw. Think of it as a kind of eddy or whirlpool in a fast-moving river. It creates a pattern that feeds upon itself and can become stronger as the waters flow around it, sucking in more and more energy from the surrounding flow."

"Well, sure," said Jeff, "but eventually a whirlpool like that will dissipate back into the normal flow of the river."

"Yes, that is what always happens eventually, but consider the red spot of Jupiter," Crullmar said. "That's an eddy discovered over four hundred years ago, and it's still going strong."

"Jupiter? A massive gas planet?" said Peter. "That spot could contain what, a thousand earths or something? Are you suggesting we're up against something that massive?"

"No," said Crullmar. "We're up against something much, much more massive. I don't think we've even felt but a small percentage of the force that's out there."

"What does that say about Jhona? About sending her out there?" Peter looked like he was just beginning to grasp the enormity of what Crullmar was saying. "How do we keep her safe?"

"Safety will only come from knowledge. As it has throughout all time," said Crullmar. "We need to understand what happened to the second talisman. If we can find it, it'll give Jhona even more power. She might even be able to eliminate the dark energy that is powering the other side.

"Let's start with some additional basic research. We know that all of the bullets Oswald fired were recovered and safely placed in the national archives. The question is…what happened to the bullet that killed Oswald? Jeff, you packed your laptop. Can you open it and do a search on that?"

"Sure, doc." Jeff removed his laptop from his bag and sat down at the little desk. In a few minutes he looked up from the screen. "It doesn't look like anyone really cared about that bullet. There are tons of comments, speculation and theories about the rounds that killed Kennedy. And I mean lots of theories, but I have a copy of the actual Oswald autopsy report. There's nothing that indicates they even bothered to remove the slug from his body. There are some pictures of Oswald's back, and it looks like the bullet fragmented. There are some small exit wounds there.

"Unless it totally fragmented, I would guess that biggest part of the bullet is still lodged in Oswald's corpse."

"Great," said Peter. "How do we get access to that?"

"Hey. Wait a minute," Jeff said. "Wow. Look. I've got an article here that says Oswald was actually dug up in 1981. Is that wild? It was done because of some crackpot theory that the big O wasn't actually buried in that grave, but it contained a Russian secret agent instead. Oswald's wife, Marina, wanted to make sure, so she signed the order."

"Dug up? Who was dug up?" It was a sleepy-looking Jhona wrapped in her comforter and now sitting up, her eyes barely open.

"Oswald, Jhona. Oswald was dug up," said Jeff. "Seriously, Dude. What a crazy…"

"Why do we care about a bunch of idiots digging up a…" said Jhona as she got up and walked over to Jeff to peer at his screen. "Ew, that's gross. Is that his body? What did they do? Totally cut him open and then sew him up like a baseball or something?"

"Yes, Jhona. That's exactly what they do after an autopsy," said Peter as he walked over to the computer. "Looks like they didn't care about doing a neat job, either. Look at that entrance wound in his chest! Even I could tell you what killed the guy. Why even bother cutting him open like that? Dude, they were just going through the motions. It must be so totally radical to be a coroner. I mean to do that all day long…"

"Hey, that's not even the cool part," said Jeff. "You heard what I said, right? They buried him in 1963 and then dug the dude back up in 1981 to confirm that it really was the O-Dude. They said all they really needed was the dude's head in order to check his dental records. One guy said that the head was actually just rolling around in the coffin. Is that cold or what?"

"Look, there are even pictures of the original coffin," said Peter. "It's all deteriorated with weird crap everywhere. Take a look. What is that covering the bottom?"

"It looks like straw or some kind of stuffing," said Jeff.

"Look, here's a picture of Oswald in the original coffin. See, there's a white kind of lining surrounding him. So he would be all comfy, I guess," said Peter.

"Yeah. Real important that the dude be all comfy when he's dead. So, it looks like water really got to it. Everything is just unrecognizable," Jeff said.

"That's right, they had to put him in a new coffin to rebury the dude," said Peter.

"Jeff, find out what happened to that original coffin." Crullmar and Samantha walked over to the computer.

"Oh, Dude, this just gets better all the time," said Jeff as he scrolled down looking at more stories. "Look, here's an article from 2010. So the old deteriorated wooden coffin was put into storage at the mortuary. After a while I guess they tried to figure out what to do with it, so these dudes actually dragged it out and sold it at an auction. Can you believe this? Some jerkoff bought this disgusting piece of crap for, like, thousands of dollars. It was described as an important historical artifact."

"Some dudes will buy anything," said Peter. "Can you imagine going to dinner at this dude's house and being asked if you want to see an historical artifact and being shown this mess?"

"That would certainly take care of dinner," said Jeff.

"I'm betting that's where we'll find the bullet," said Crullmar. "As the whole mess deteriorated the bullet likely just fell to the bottom of the box. It could still be there."

"Unless one of the jerkoffs found it," said Jeff.

"Yeah. Unless one of the jerkoffs found it…" said Crullmar, his voice trailing off.

"Wait a minute, Joe," said Annabelle. "What if it fell out of the casket onto the ground when they were digging it up? They probably wouldn't even have noticed it."

"Yes, that's another possibility," said Crullmar. It would be a lot easier to search the gravesite than to try to find the old casket."

"Quite a lot easier," said Jeff. "The proud new owner decided to remain anonymous."

"Is this like that old joke where the guy loses his keys, but insists on looking for them under a streetlight because the light is better than in the dark corner where he actually lost them?" said Peter.

"Exactly like that, except for one thing," said Samantha. "We've got something the guy under the streetlight didn't have."

Everyone turned and looked at Jhona.

"Me? You want to send *me* back down that rabbit hole? Well forget it. I get a goddamn migraine every time I do it—not to mention the runs, and I think my period is starting."

"Your period?" asked Samantha. "Are you on time?"

"Fuck no. I'm almost two weeks early."

"What are your symptoms, sweetie?"

"Oh, sure, Samantha, like I'm going to discuss all that in front of everyone."

"I understand, dear, but this could be very important. Will you talk to Annabelle and me in the bedroom? In private?"

"Oh sure. I'd just love to do that, *dearie*. Let's go. I can hardly wait…"

As the women retreated into the bedroom, Jeff gave Peter a look and said, "I'd add crabbiness to that list of symptoms."

"Not funny, Dude," said Peter. "Not one goddamn bit funny."

THERE AINT NO CURE

After a good hour when Samantha emerged from the bedroom, she looked like she was about to deliver some bad news. She walked over to the mini bar, removed a beer and took three deep swallows.

"Jhona's bleeding has me concerned. I don't know what is going on with her, but if I had to guess, which I suppose I do, I'd say the tidal forces caused by the interference patterns are literally trying to tear her apart. It's not her period. In magic, women are more effective…more deadly, but more vulnerable than men, and Jhona is up against both Oswald and Ruby—both men, or the essence of men anyway.

"Women like Jhona can effectively wield the energy patterns caused by the interference patterns, but they are open to being corrupted by them. Our little Jhona is becoming a mighty warrior, something she is really starting to revel in. On the other hand she wants her normal life back. This is creating a personal conflict that weakens her resolve and can limit her effectiveness at a time when she might need to be most effective."

"So what do you suggest we do?" asked Crullmar.

"We need to use her very sparingly. No more séances unless there is no other way. We can't afford to think of her as a tool, or more appropriately a weapon.

"Our next step in this is to find the bullet if we can without using her. Joe, she should stay here with Peter while the rest of us can go to the gravesite and take a look around. We might get lucky."

"Samantha, are you really suggesting that the dark forces we're dealing with involve Oswald and Ruby?" asked Crullmar.

"Well, at this point, it looks that way to me. One theory suggests that when people conduct violent acts in their lifetimes, their spirits are forced to remain in our Holographic plane and work to resolve the karmic issues.

"I think their two spirits are engaged in a kind of "danse macabre" with Ruby as the aggressive one trying to crush Oswald with direct power. Oswald, true to his character, is effusive, striking from a distance and then retreating.

"From what we've experienced, both of Ruby's talismans were generated by Ruby's actions. The bullet that took Oswald's life, and the tape that contains his confession. Both of those wouldn't be all that remarkable from a supernatural point of view, except for Ruby's comments about demons.

"Ruby knew he was being possessed, but not forced to do anything he didn't want to. I'd say that is the most important aspect of what he said. It's more like he was aided by these dark forces, inspired by them perhaps, but not forced. He acted with a will, and that will is still lodged in the Holographic interference patterns. It's kind of like Crullmar's description of a persistent eddy in a swift river.

"I think the talismans are providing the dark energy that keep the eddies moving.

"Samantha, what about Oswald? How does he play in all this?" asked Crullmar as Annabelle and Jhona emerged from the bedroom.

"Well, I'm not sure, but as I talk about it I become less sure that Oswald is really involved. I think the opposing force is driven more by the idea of Oswald, an idea usurped by someone—another witch, perhaps. I wish I knew more about that so called library assistant who disappeared after you played the tape, the one who looked like Oswald."

"What is the *idea of Oswald*?" asked Jhona. "That just sounds like so much double talk."

"It's the idea that the assassin has the power to change the course of history. That's really the power to change the future in a dramatic way. What's especially appealing to some people is that it can be done by a single person, acting alone, believing he's doing it for the good of society."

"They always believe that, don't they?" asked Jeff.

"Yes, they always do," answered Samantha.

"I don't understand something, Samantha," Jhona asked. "Why wouldn't Oswald's force be part of it, too, instead of just Ruby's?"

"That's probably because Oswald's force was cancelled by Ruby. Oswald killed JFK by force and then died by the same kind of force. It was retribution, a kind of cancellation of negative forces," said Samantha.

"Well, Ruby died, too…" said Jeff.

"Yes, but not violently," said Crullmar. "In fact he was in the process of getting a new trial, so technically he wasn't even guilty of the crime."

"I had no idea that this stuff actually lingers in the, what is it? The nether world," asked Peter.

"Well, it does. At least until it gets cancelled out," explained Samantha.

BULLETS CARRY THE NEWS

"We've got to find out what is going on at Oswald's gravesite," said Crullmar. "Jeff, see if you can find the location of his grave on the Internet."

Two seconds later Jeff responded, "He is buried at Shannon Rose Hill Memorial Burial Park in Fort Worth."

"Good lord what did we ever do before the Internet?" said Crullmar.

"This USA Today article says the gravesite is a major tourist attraction," said Jeff.

"That's good," Crullmar said. "We can pose as tourists by taking a lot of goofy pictures with our smart phones. Look, Samantha, I know you don't want to involve Jhona any more than is necessary, but she's probably the only one among us who can feel the interference patterns caused by the bullet if it is still at the grave site."

"Okay, Joe, but I'm liking all this less and less."

"Jhona? What about it? Are you up to a field trip to Oswald's gravesite? It's not all that far from here," asked Crullmar.

"Sure. Why not? What's the worst that can happen? Well, let's see…I could get sucked up into the many, crazy interference patterns that I see each time I venture down that rabbit hole. That's one thing.

"Oh, wait. I know I'll get pulverized by that other witch who has been dogging me each time I go there. In case you've forgotten, that's the guy? Entity? Whatever, who almost blew apart the magic circle that was supposed to protect me. That could happen."

"Jhona," said Peter. "We've got to bring this thing to a conclusion. Otherwise you'll be haunted for the rest of your life."

"Haunted. That's a great word for it. Haunted. You know what? I don't give a flying fuck. Let that little prick, whoever he is, try one of his little magic tricks. I don't think he, or any of you for that matter, have any idea how strong I've become."

No one had anything to add to that statement, but Samantha thought she saw a quick spark flare up behind Jhona's eyes. Just for an instant. It was unsettling, and it made Samantha shiver for an instant.

The next morning they all had breakfast together at the hotel café. There wasn't much conversation, and after everyone had finished, Peter went to the concierge to arrange for a car rental. Jeff accompanied him to buy some snacks and bottled water for the excursion. He purchased goofy looking sun hats, sunglasses and belly packs to top off the tourist look. He also bought some cheap flowers.

They all waited outside for Peter and Jeff to drive up. "We look like a bunch of dumb-ass German tourists," said Jhona. "I hope to God I don't see anyone I know."

"You know people in Texas?" asked Annabelle.

"Not yet," she answered. "But I'll bet I'm going to meet some really fascinating people before the day ends."

An anonymous white van pulled up, and Peter got out.

"Great," said Jhona. "A *van*. It just gets better." It wasn't even ten a.m. yet, but it was as hot as a back-alley blowjob, thought Jhona. She could feel herself getting cross. That was a term her mother used, and Jhona hated it. Well, she hated just about everything this morning, which was a fact. She became aware that Peter was motioning for her to get in the van.

He was always a gentleman to her, and he took her arm to help her up into it. She shook it off and said, "I'm not riding in the back...unless you want this piece of shit van covered in barf."

"Okay, Jhona," he said. "Whatever you need to do."

She got in, hating it more and more each second.

BABY CAN YOU DRIVE MY CAR

On the drive out to the cemetery in Fort Worth, Jeff, looking on his smart phone, found several Internet sites that gave valuable information on Oswald's gravesite. First was some information about how the cemetery staff refuses to give directions to the gravesite. That wasn't a problem, because the site gave detailed directions.

As the van entered the cemetery gates, Crullmar gave some last-minute instructions to the group. "All we're going to do here is pretend we are curious tourists. We'll be left alone as long as we take photos. We can bend down to place flowers and small stones, which is a Jewish tradition."

"Who's Jewish in this crowd besides me?" asked Jhona.

"You're missing the point, Jhona. The stones and flowers just give us an excuse to bend down and examine the soil," said Crullmar. "About the only thing we won't be able to do is dig."

"Yeah, that would look a little suspicious, wouldn't it?" chucked Jeff.

"Will I be able to prostrate myself onto the grave and sob for a while?" said Jhona.

"Whatever makes you happy, girlfriend," said Annabelle. "I'm sure Ozzy would just love it if you did."

That brought a little smile to Jhona's lips. Peter placed his hand on her knee, and gave it a little squeeze.

"Both hands on the wheel, buster," she said.

LET'S DANCE

The little group found the entrance to the cemetery and drove slowly and respectively through the gates past the administration building. A polite wave from Peter was returned with a nod and a half smile from one of the black-suited officials milling around the building.

Making their way over to the western area of the park, they had no problem finding the, red granite marker that said, simply, "Oswald." This was the grave of a man who needed no introduction.

Referencing one of his websites, Jeff explained that the original headstone had been replaced with this simple version after the original marker had been stolen.

"Stolen?" asked Jhona. "Who would do something like that?"

"Teenagers," said Jeff. "They stole it four years to the day of the JFK assassination. The original marker's ownership is still in dispute."

With that, the van came to a stop just across from the marker. It was located in a flat, depressing section of the cemetery. Even the grass didn't look happy. It seemed like the kind of place where Fort Worth's lower echelon came to rest. There were a few flowers scattered across some of the plots, and the weeds seemed to be kept under control. *"That was something at least,"* thought Jhona.

The group gingerly approached the marker. They could see a couple of the black suits watching them from the administration building. They were too far away to actually see their expressions, but it didn't take too much imagination to know they were suspicious.

Crullmar guessed that a lot of weird people had gathered here over the years. None of them were nearly as weird as this little group.

"Jhona, why don't you take that bouquet of flowers from Peter and get down on your knees," said Crullmar.

"Move your hands over the dirt. See if you can pick up anything."

"What am I?" she said. "Some kind of goddamn human metal detector?"

"No, not metal, more like vortices, interference patterns in the Hologram."

TO SERVE AND PROTECT

As soon as Jhona placed her hands on the grave they began tingling—as though they had fallen asleep. The tingling was stronger in her right hand, and Jhona could see it was turning black again.

"Christ. Here we go again," she thought.

"Quick. Hold hands and make a circle around her," said Samantha.

Jhona tried to push herself up, but her hands were beginning to sink into the earth. Dorothy began emerging from Jhona's right hand, the black one. Dorothy was saying something as she, too, began sinking into the grave. She had a look of panic on her face. Jhona couldn't hear what she was saying, and her face was too distorted for Jhona to read her lips.

Jhona looked up right before her head was about to sink into the loam. She saw a dark figure looking at them, the same one from her last encounter.

Her circle of friends was being absorbed into the grave, as though it were made of quicksand. They were screaming, up to their waists in the grave.

For a second Jhona stopped moving into the grave. Her chin was just barely above the grass. The dark figure was approaching…walking very casually. She knew who it was even before she could see him clearly. Oswald!

She could hear the screams seeming to come from far away. "Jhona," they were saying. "Use your power."

It wasn't time for that yet. First she had to confront the Oswald. She calmly watched him saunter closer to the grave. He looked exactly like a Hologram. His image was shifting through all the photographs taken of him. First he was in his Marine uniform, holding a rifle, going through the Marine rifle drill, which consisted of waiving the rifle around like he was in some kind of perverted drill team.

He was about ten feet from Jhona now, but she knew that was just an illusion. No Hologram was really located in space. Then he began morphing into the famous backyard photos taken by his poor wife, Marina.

As always, the smirk was on the smartass face. He alternated between holding the rifle and then holding a banjo. He started strumming away, dancing like a minstrel, his feet bouncing like he's some sort of wooden, dancing puppet.

His Hologram, smartass face leaned down to within an inch of Jhona's face. She could smell his fetid breath. It was the smell of a corpse.

Now, Jhona's companions were completely absorbed by the grave. She knew she was alone, totally alone. Even Dorothy was gone now.

"Fuck you, you goddamn pervert asshole mother fucker," Jhona yelled. It's time now. Jhona was not afraid. She was pissed. She tried to raise her arms, but they were pinioned by all the dirt. She couldn't move them.

Then the corpse face was actually rubbing against Jhona's cheek. It was partially decomposed, but amazingly enough the smirk was still there. Jhona tried to move away, but she was still pinioned. The smell was overwhelming. Jhona desperately wanted to close her eyes, but that would be giving up, and she had never been the type to…

Then came the tongue. It was black from decomposition and looked more reptile than human, which was no surprise to Jhona. There's never been anything human about Oswald, not really, anyway.

The tongue was forked, and one end started going up her nose while the other end tried to enter her mouth. She kept her teeth tightly clamped in defiance. The tongue was probing, probing, insistent; the smirk took on a triumphant look.

Suddenly she became aware that she was holding the tape with her right arm. *Where the hell did that come from?* she thought. Her arm began moving upward.

Then she noticed Dorothy drifting up from the grave. Oswald was distracted for a moment, and the tongue hesitated for an instant. Dorothy was holding something, something shiny, bright, glowing like a coal. It was the bullet.

Jhona opened her mouth and clamped down hard onto the tongue totally severing the tip. She could feel the tip squirming in her mouth like a worm.

Oswald recoiled, the smartass smirk replaced with a look of surprise and fear. He was afraid of the bullet. Dorothy was completely out of the grave now, waving the bullet around in her hand. Her face less decomposed now. Jhona could make out what she was saying even though there were no sounds. "Want some, Ozzy Rabbit? Want some?"

Jhona spit out the squirming piece of tongue. As it hit the dirt it burst into a flash and was gone.

Oswald turned on Dorothy and threw his banjo at her. It turned into *the* rifle. It was in mid-air when Dorothy threw the bullet. The two collided and disappeared. Oswald began drifting over to where Dorothy was floating. She was helpless now; never really was much of a witch.

But Jhona *was* a witch, a very *powerful* witch. With every bit of strength she had, she pulled both of her arms free, and then her legs. She was standing now looking at Oswald's back as he drifted toward Dorothy.

"Ozzy Rabbit," she shouted. She knew somehow it was a magic name. What they called him in the Marines. "Ooooozzzzzzyyyy. Ozzy Rabbit. Little, Ozzy Rabbit wouldn't hurt a flea, little tiny Ozzy Rabbit."

Oswald turned to face her, immense hatred on his face. He was capable of so much destruction. He changed the world, didn't he? Fucking changed it beyond all recognition. He's—not—afraid—of—a—god—damn—girl.

Jhona raised her hands. "Every bit, every little bit, every god damn little bit," she began chanting. She thrust out her hands. The shock wave was terrible, all encompassing. It changed everything. Everything.

EVERY LITTLE BIT OF EVERYTHING

Dorothy liked reading the Sunday paper before getting her hair done. Every other day of the week she had to get up early. There were always people to interview. Keeping up a daily column was not an easy thing to do. She had to keep what seemed like a million stories in her mind each day, and she always had to look for the little tidbits that other journalists missed.

She opened the paper to the national news section letting the rest of the paper drop to her bed. It made a delightful mess that she found very comforting somehow.

Here was something…in Dallas…a local strip club owner shoots a former Marine who had lived in Russia for two years. No reason given. A random killing? It might be interesting to interview the guy…find out what was going through his head. She made a mental note to check it out first thing Monday morning. You just never know. Could turn into something really interesting.

The End

About the Author:

W.H. Matlack is a prolific writer of novels, short stories, and graphic stories (OK, comic books). He lives in the San Francisco Bay Area with his wife and two cats.

Social Media Links:

Facebook: https://www.facebook.com/william.h.matlack?fref=ts

www.ingramcontent.com/pod-product-compliance
Lightning Source LLC
Chambersburg PA
CBHW051644260626
47170CB00004B/1324